Also by Douglas Hackney

How the World Works
601 Thoughts on Life, Work and Business

Data Marts
Understanding and Implementing Successful Data Marts

The Next Name

The

Next Name

Douglas Hackney

Published by Amboy Media
Houston, Texas, U.S.A.

First Edition
First Printing 2008 / 12

ISBN-13 978-0-9821719-3-6
ISBN-10 0-9821719-3-5

Library of Congress Control Number: 2008909223

Front and back cover illustrations reprinted by permission of Agustín Llagostera

Cover design: Douglas Hackney
Pukara de Quitor illustrations: Douglas Hackney

Printed in the United States of America

For Adam

Pukara de Quitor
Top View

The South
The Way of the Falcon

The
West

The Way
of the
Condor

120 meters / 393 feet

200 meters / 656 feet

The North
The Way of the Gods

The
East

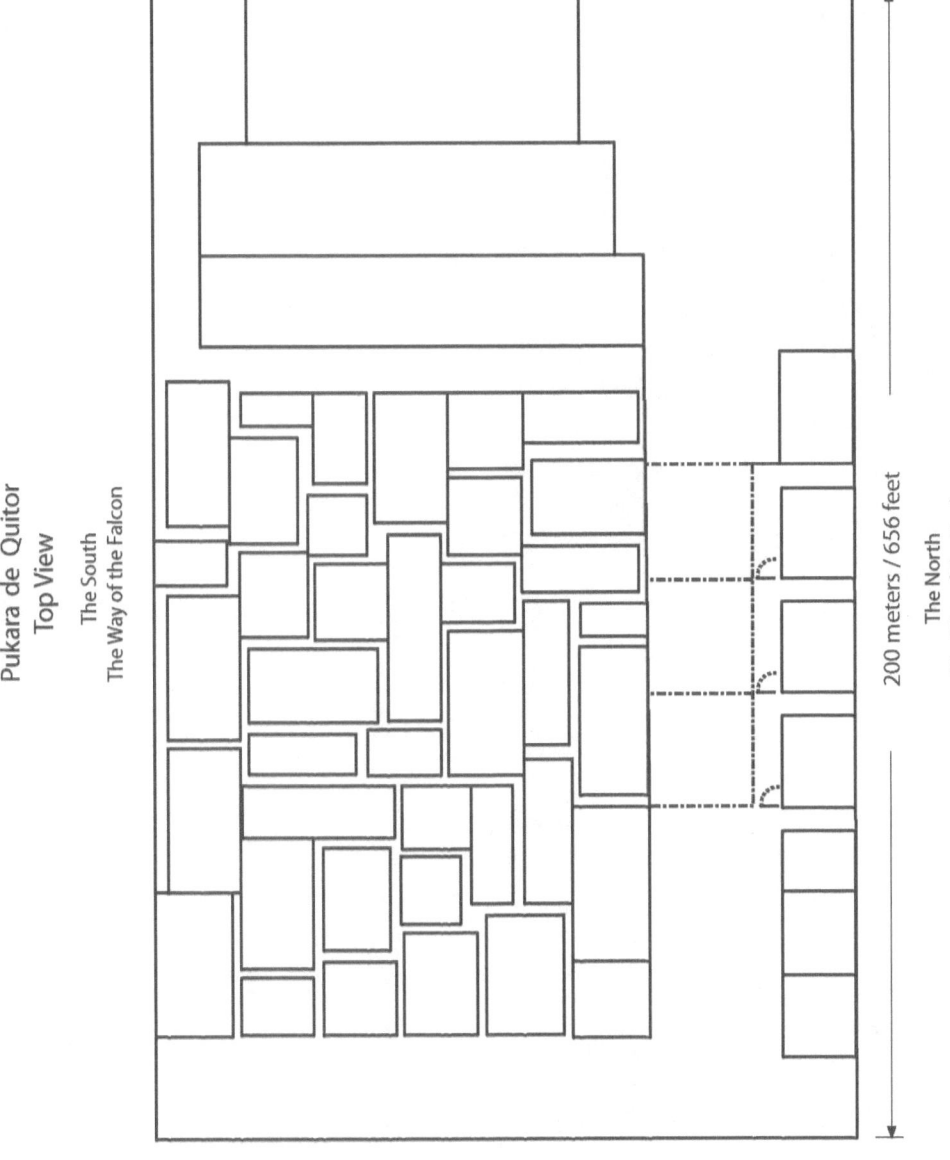

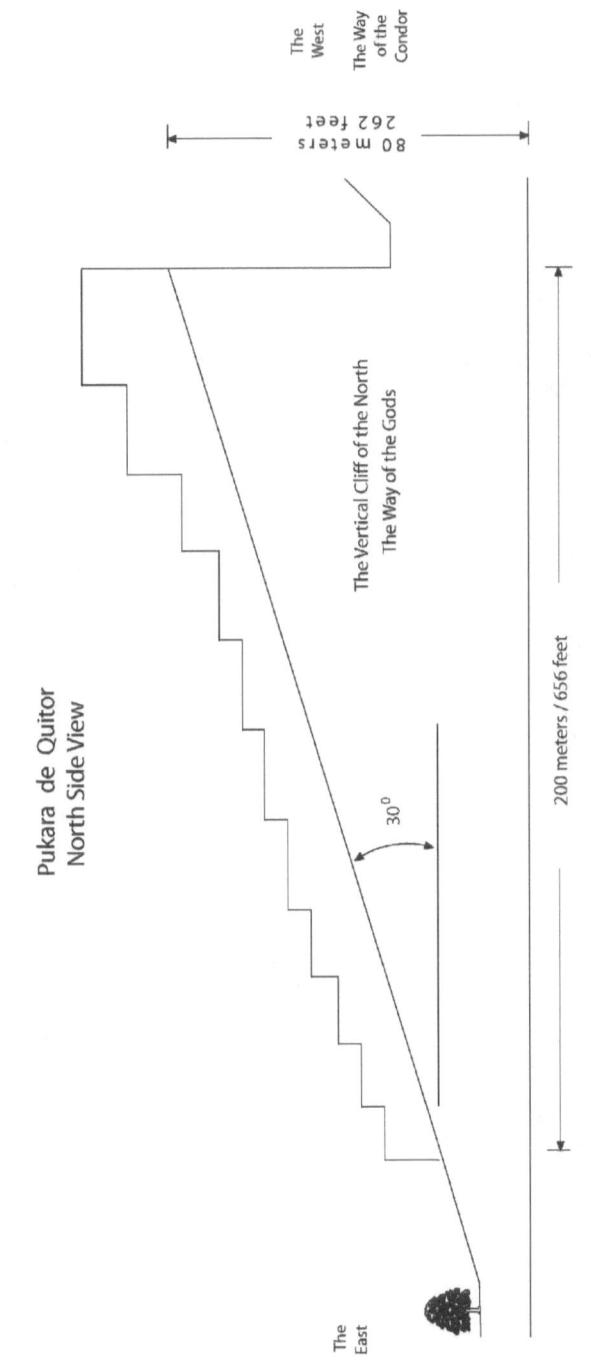

Pukara de Quitor
North Side View

The East

The West

The Way
of the Condor

The Vertical Cliff of the North
The Way of the Gods

80 meters
262 feet

200 meters / 656 feet

30°

Table of Contents

Preface

From the beginning of their conquest and subjugation of the New World, the Spanish Conquistadors defeated every enemy and toppled every civilization that stood in their path. No ruler could defy them, no army defeat them, and no fortress withstand them.

That all changed when the Spanish encountered the Atacameños, a small civilization centered around an oasis in the driest desert on the planet in what is now northeastern Chile.

The Atacameños defeated the Spanish twice, first in 1536 and again in 1540. For the Spanish, the defeats were unprecedented insults and challenges to their power. No one, anywhere, from Mexico to Peru, had successfully defied the Conquistadors.

For the Atacameños and their stronghold, the Pukara de Quitor (Fortress of Quitor), the Spanish defeats were merely two more battles in their undefeated history. Just as the Spanish had been virtually undefeated in their conquest of the New World, the Atacameños and the Pukara de Quitor had never been conquered by any enemy.

The Next Name

The Spanish returned to the Pukara de Quitor for their third attempt at victory later in 1540, this time augmented by Incas.

The resulting battle was the climactic confrontation of three great civilizations: the European Spanish, destined to rule for hundreds of years; the Inca, former rulers of an empire of more than 12 million people; and the Atacameños, at more than 2,500 years one of the world's oldest continuous civilizations, and until then, undefeated and unconquered.

One day in 1540, the Spanish, Inca and Atacameños met in battle.

This is the story of that fateful day.

One

The King waited for the tray and tube. His were the most ornate of all the elites, more delicately carved and decorated than any other. And, since the Inca's collapse, they no longer reflected the Inca sun cult. The motif now was a return to the Atacameños cosmology; the familiar Gods had returned.

The attendants raised the tray, carefully placed the tube, and the King inhaled the dream powder. Its familiar effects were instantaneous.

The King raised his arms and slowly rotated. His entire inner court, senior commanders, cadre of high priests, and royal family circled him. He looked deeply into each set of eyes. He looked for confirmation of fealty. He looked for confirmation of faith. And today, he looked for confirmation of courage.

The King finished his rotation back to the east and closed his eyes. He waited for the morning's dream, the morning's vision, the morning's direct message from the Gods.

He saw the coming battle. It would be today. He saw the southern wall. He saw it under attack.

He always knew it would be the South, the only place the fortress had ever been threatened.

The visions flickered and flashed. Battle. Blood. South. And then, near the end, the last vision was the Condor, the highest deity, the god of two faces, two messages.

The King welcomed the Condor. It spoke to him of power, of the highest possible place, circling the sky, the intermediary between this life and the next. The Condor was the guardian, ever watching. The Condor would watch today.

As the vision ended, the sun's first rays appeared at the winter mark, the northernmost point of its annual march.

The priests murmured, their bi-annual calculations confirmed.

Chapter One

On his elevated dais, the King received the first rays. The intense golden light illuminated his plates of gold and trimming of iridescent tropical feathers. In the seconds it took the sun to light him, he grew in stature and power.

Elevated on the royal terrace, on the highest building in the mountain fortress, he shone like a beacon, and glimmered like a god.

All those in the walled city turned to him and shouted their praise.

He was their King. He was their god here on earth. He saw all through the dream powder. He knew all through his blood.

The King began the speaking of the names.

He began with the first name, the first King, the first to unite the tribes.

He spoke each name forcefully, so the entire city could hear. He spoke strongly, so his voice carried beyond the high, impenetrable walls, so the enemy could hear.

"Let them hear the names," the King thought. "Let them hear the names of our kings, more than 2,500 years of kings. Let them know what they face—a people, a tribe, a civilization that has never known failure. Let them know they face a fortress that has never been breached, a people that have never been defeated. Let them hear the names."

The names echoed the Atacameños history: from hunter-gatherers to the first farmers; from simple farming to surplus crops; from surplus crops to multiple classes; from multiple classes to craftspeople; from craftspeople to trading with local tribes; from trading with local tribes to an expanding kingdom; from an expanding kingdom to dominion over the entire Atacama; from dominion of the Atacama to trading with regional empires; from trading with regional empires to integration with them; from integration with regional empires to surviving them; from surviving them to becoming the oldest continuous civilization in the known world.

The names ended with him, the King, the Atacameños King.

As his name echoed across the valley, the people of the fortress again roared accolades.

The King soaked it in, absorbing the power of the affirmations.

These were his people, this was his land—undefiled, undefeated, unconquered—as it was today, as it would be evermore.

The King raised his arms to his people and spoke.

"Atacameños! You have heard the names. You have heard 2,500 years of kings. Those kings built and defended this kingdom. Those kings built and defended this mighty fortress. Those kings defeated every enemy, just as this King will defeat the enemy outside our gates today. We have endured, and we will endure. We will endure another 2,500 years! None shall defeat the Atacameños! None shall breach the Pukara de Quitor!"

The roar rising from the fortress below was deafening. The people were ready.

The King received the adulation, lowered his arms, and turned to his high council.

"It will be the South!" the King proclaimed. "I have seen it. The Condor himself brought it to me."

A chorus of assent rippled through the council.

"Concentrate the defenses on the South, near the Sacrificador," ordered the King.

"It will be so," replied his generals.

"The Tiwanakus may have come close there, but these foreigners and their Inca slaves will fail there, fail like all the others who have challenged

Pukara de Quitor. None shall breach this fortress!" the King roared to his council. "Go, prepare the fortress! The battle will be today!"

The generals scurried off the platform, shouting the commands of battle to their seconds.

The King turned to his son, the crown Prince, and asked, "Any word from our spy?"

"He did not return before sunrise," his eldest son replied.

The King's brows knotted. "That is unfortunate," he confided to his son. "His stories yesterday of the Inca slaves being promised all the treasures of our kingdom, all the lands of our kingdom, all the women of our kingdom, were so outrageous. Why do you think the foreigners would make such promises to slaves?"

"Only to break them," replied his son. "The Incas are now weak-minded, ready to believe anything that promises an easier life. They have nothing; they are a broken people, mere slaves to the foreigners."

The Prince took a step forward towards his father.

Chapter One

"Father, we are not the Incas," the Prince declared. "We have not forgotten what built this impregnable fortress. We have not forgotten what built our kingdom. We know the names."

The King put his hands on his son's shoulders.

"My son," the King asserted, "you will be a fine King. The blood of the Atacameños kings runs strong in you. Tomorrow, you will lead your people well. But today, you will lead the most critical defense of this war, the South. Put your strength and the oils at the Sacrificador. I have seen the vision. The battle will be there."

"Yes, my King," replied his son, stepping back. "We will triumph! The Pukara de Quitor will repel all once again. None shall breach this fortress!" The Prince turned and strode away to the sounds of the drums of battle. The movement of warriors and supplies to the South had already begun.

The King turned to the eastern forest, to the enemy camp. His oldest and most trusted advisor joined him. The sun was up and lit the entire fortress city and the green oasis valley that lay below.

"What do you make of the roofs?" his advisor asked.

"We hoped to learn that today, but our spy did not return," replied the King.

"They are a strange construction," commented the advisor. "They are a roof with no building underneath. They have stacks and stacks of them. And, they've been working under them on the base of the East for days. Our arrows have proven ineffective against the roofs there."

"None shall breach the East," the King snapped. "The names have invested centuries in building the East. It is the Pukara de Quitor's only man-made defense."

The King turned to face the advisor, his voice rising, "The North, a sheer cliff more than 50 men high; the West, another cliff; the South, a deep ravine topped by a cliff; all were provided by the Gods for our protection. Only the East was man's responsibility. It was the duty of the names to build and protect the East. None shall breach the East!"

"Yes, my lord, of course, none shall breach the East," replied the advisor obsequiously.

At that moment great shouts arose from the enemy camp outside the eastern wall. The King and his advisor turned toward the sounds. Two foreigners mounted on their giant beasts came forward. An Inca walked beside them. One foreigner raised his arm and the enemy camp grew silent.

The Inca shouted in the Atacameños's Kunzan tongue, "King, we have someone with a message for you. But he will have difficulty talking to you."

With that, the Inca threw something at the east wall, falling far short of clearing it.

"That was his tongue," shouted the Inca. "And here is his head." He raised a long pike with the spy's head mounted on top. There was a low groan from the fortress, followed by a shrieking scream.

"Quiet his woman!" ordered the King. An orderly ran down the stairs to find and silence the spy's wife.

The Inca raised another pike and shouted, "King, this pike is for your head! Your head will be on it by the end of this day!"

He turned and shouted the same message in the Quechuan tongue to the Inca slaves. They roared in approval, the blood lust of battle building in their throats.

"Summon the generals," the King ordered, and turned away from the Inca and the foreigners.

As the generals gathered, the King turned again to his most senior advisor.

"I know that Inca," the King declared.

"Yes," replied the advisor. "I remember him too. He was the Administrator in Catarpe, but he disappeared soon after the Inca collapse. And, if I remember correctly, he was hosted here in Pukara de Quitor and toured the fortress."

"That is unfortunately the case," replied the King. "He and his family visited here often. Our children played together. His son and the little Prince both fell off the garden wall together. His daughter and the younger Princess planted a cactus in the Princess's garden. It was their friendship cactus, to bind them together for all time."

"Does he know all?" the advisor interrupted.

"He does not know all, but he knows enough," replied the King.

The generals finally arrived. The General of the East took the longest, having made the long climb up the twisting pathways of the fortress.

Chapter One

"Generals," began the King, "we face today another threat to our fortress, to our lands, to our civilization, to our way of life.

"The names, the ancients, faced these threats, and defeated all who threatened. We, together, have faced these threats before. We, together, have twice defeated these same foreigners, the last time less than one year ago.

"As we learned in the first and second battle with them, these foreigners are not Gods. We have seen them bleed in battle. They are men—pale, white men who melt before our sun.

"They are not of this land. They cannot survive in this land. They cannot survive because it is our land!

"We are the Atacameños! We are the sons of the names! Victory is our destiny!"

The generals raised their fists and shouted, "Victory!"

As the generals turned to leave, the King pulled his son aside and asked, "Are the defenses of the South ready?"

"We are waiting on the last of the oil from the East, but otherwise we are ready. We have most of the warriors in position," the Prince replied.

"Good, go and repeat to the warriors what I told the Generals," the King commanded. "Remind them that the foreigners are not Gods, but men. We will defeat them today as we defeated them twice before."

"Yes, my King!" his son responded. He turned and returned to the South.

"King, behold, your vision is confirmed," the advisor proclaimed, pointing towards the Southeast.

The King looked out and saw foreigners and Inca slaves moving towards the ravine that cut up the mountain along the south side of the fortress, far below the cliff and southern wall.

"Yes, the Condor brings the truth," the King replied confidently.

"Isn't it remarkable, the power and duration of history," the King commented to his advisor. "It has been more than 1,000 years since the Tiwanakus merely threatened a breach of the South, but that legend lives on, the knowledge lives on, even among our enemies."

"That knowledge is nowhere more clear and vibrant than among our enemies, my King," replied the advisor.

"And, look," the King commented while pointing to the enemy. "The Inca slaves are bringing the roofs. We shall finally see what the foreigners do with a roof with no building in open battle. What fool would build a roof with no building?"

"And, what hubris," added the advisor. "The foreigners are as small a force as they were the first two times we defeated them. I count no more foreigners than they came with four years ago and returned with earlier this very year."

"The only difference I see is the Inca slaves," agreed the King. "And what good will they be? Even though there are indeed hoards of them, you can plainly see from their dress they are but peasants and farmers. Look at the front ranks; they put the lowliest in the fore! What army puts their poorest assets at the head of battle? These foreigners conduct war in very strange ways."

"Perhaps they were seduced by their easy success with the Incas," offered the advisor. "The Incas were so weak and soft from self-indulgence and shattered by their civil war of philosophies and arms that they crumbled with merely a tap. The foreigners may assume that all civilizations are the same, ready to fall with the slightest provocation."

"The Incas were destroyed by their own affluence," the King insisted. "They reached their peak of power and immediately forgot what their empire, their success, was built on. They forgot what created it, what was required to sustain it. They turned to a life of self-indulgence, expectation, and entitlement. Instead of building and sustaining their civilization, they turned upon each other. The two warring camps destroyed everything for the sake of their faction. They sacrificed the whole empire for their selfish, narrow self-interests.

"Within less than three generations, less than three kings, less than three names after their peak, the entire Inca civilization was enslaved. Their treasure was stolen, their women were raped, and their children now die in the silver mines. Their lives are over, just like their civilization.

"Look at them before us, tattered, beaten, and defeated. How many of them died on the forced march to our kingdom? They are fools, these Inca slaves. The foreigners will slaughter them after this battle regardless of the outcome. The only treasure and women the slaves will see is in paradise." The King spat out the last words with disgust.

"As we proved we were superior to the Tiwanaku, we proved ourselves superior to the Inca," the advisor proclaimed, gazing over the Inca slaves entering the southern ravine. "Like the Tiwanaku before them, the Inca helped us expand our trade, which grew our wealth. And, even with their tributes, the Inca proved to be a net financial gain for our kingdom. But, unlike the Tiwanaku and Inca, we, the Atacameños, never lost sight of the most important goal of our lives and of our civilization: to extend the list of names."

"You are indeed wise, my friend," the King affirmed, placing his hand upon the advisor's shoulder.

"Come," the King summoned, his manner brightening, "the battle begins. We shall watch the foreigners fail again and witness the sad fate of the Inca slaves. We will feast tomorrow to celebrate the sun's return to its southern journey, another victory for the impregnable Pukara de Quitor, and the eldest Princess's wedding."

The Next Name

Two

From the southwest corner of the royal terrace the King and his advisor watched the clouds of dust from the south ravine. They could no longer see the foreigners or the Inca slaves because the enemy was far below the wall and the cliff, but they could see the Atacameños sentries on the wall.

Each sentry along the South raised his hand to reflect the progress of the enemy force. The enemy doggedly climbed up the ravine, making steady progress. Hand by hand, the King measured their climb up the mountain. The sentry at the statue of the Sacrificador was the last to raise his hand. The enemy stopped. The battle would be joined there.

"Just as you predicted!" exclaimed the advisor. "They attack at the Sacrificador! It is indeed the South. The legend of the Tiwanaku near-breech lives on!"

"Yes, it is the South," replied the King, watching the dust cloud rise up from the ravine and boil into the sky. "The Condor delivers the truth."

The King looked down to the Sacrificador command post. His son, his treasure, his pride, the future of the kingdom, the next name, was looking up at him.

The King raised his right hand slowly, and when it was fully extended, clenched his fist.

His son replied with the same motion, and when his fist clenched, he shouted with all his strength, "Battle! To Battle! We are the Atacameños! None shall breach Pukara de Quitor!"

A roar went up from the defenders of the South, and the Atacameños warriors mounted the battlements.

The Inca slaves in the ravine replied with a roar of their own, and the first wave of Inca arrows swept up and over the south wall.

The Atacameños warriors on the wall returned a volley of arrows, which were followed by screams from the unarmored, unshielded front ranks of Inca slaves.

"They die. The poorest and the least, they die by the hundreds," mused the advisor, listening to the carnage below.

"Yes, the brutality of the foreigners is unbounded," the King assessed. "Their desire for others' blood is strong."

The advisor nodded and looked back down to the battle.

"Look there, I see the first ladder!" the advisor exclaimed.

"Indeed, they have made it to the base of the cliff," observed the King.

The crude Inca ladders were easily pushed off by the warriors on the battlements, but a few Atacameños warriors fell to the barrage of accurate Inca arrows that accompanied each attempt.

"I think that some of these peasants are not peasants after all," growled the King, with an edge to his voice.

"Yes, the archers are much too disciplined, precise and worthy to be mere peasants," replied the advisor. "One must wonder what else we see that is not what we see."

"Yes, one must wonder," the King muttered, the day's first clouds of concern gathering on his brow.

Again and again the tops of ladders appeared above the battlements. Again and again the ladders were repelled. Again and again a few Atacameños warriors fell. Again and again volleys of arrows rained down from the battlements on the Inca slaves below. Again and again waves of screams arose from the ravine.

The King watched as a runner from the battle below approached the royal terrace. A commander received the message and brought it to the King.

"My King," the commander began. "The Prince reports that our warriors are successfully repelling the ladder attacks. Hundreds of the enemy fell from our arrows. Never in our history, under any King, have we killed as many as we have already today. No enemy can sustain these losses. Our victory is imminent!"

"Thank you," replied the King. "Your service to your King is noted and most appreciated. Is there more?"

"Yes, my King," the commander elaborated. "Yes, there is more. The Prince requests permission to light the fires to finish the enemy, destroy their will, and win the battle."

The King pondered the request.

Chapter Two

Never before, under any King, for any name, had so many of the enemy fallen in battle. The slaves were dying by the hundreds. The remainder cowered in the trees of the oasis, terrified by the screams of their tribesmen perishing in the ravine.

"No enemy can withstand such losses. No army can continue to send its men to certain death. No enemy can sustain the fight against the impregnable fortress of Pukara de Quitor," the King adjudged.

The advisor nodded slightly.

"Light the fires," the King ordered the commander. "And, tell the Prince his name shall shine brightly for thousands of years."

"Yes, my King!" the commander shouted, overjoyed at the prospect of delivering the decisive command in the most glorious victory in the 2,500-year history of the Atacameños.

The runner flew back down the twisting corridors of the fortress to the Prince. Within minutes, fires raged at regular intervals along the wall of the South.

"It will take some time for them to boil," the advisor remarked.

"Yes," the King responded, as another volley of arrows flew down from the battlements onto the Inca slaves, wiping out the last of the second rank and much of the equally unprotected third.

"My King, observe the north pepper tree grove," urged the advisor, pointing over the eastern wall to the green fields between the grove and the river.

"Whatever could be of interest there, when the battle climaxes at the South?" retorted the King, anxious to see the moment of triumph in the battle of the millennium.

"My King, I beg you, turn and observe," the advisor implored.

With a disgusted huff, the King turned.

"I swear by the Gods, if it was anyone but you interrupting me now..." the King's voice trailed off.

A score of Inca slaves broke from the shade of the trees into the bright sun of the open fields lining the river. Hot in pursuit rode a mounted foreigner. His armor shone in the unrelenting desert sun, and the muscles of his giant beast rippled with each long stride.

As he overtook them, his sword flashed. One by one, he cut them down. Only when they were all grounded did he dismount. He grabbed the slave who made it the furthest, a young man now bleeding profusely from the stump of his shoulder where his left arm used to be.

The foreigner dragged the Inca slave to a rock on the riverside, pulled his head onto the rock, and decapitated him with one quick stroke. He retrieved the head with the point of his sword, mounted his beast, and rode back towards the trees with it hoisted high.

The former Inca Administrator then appeared from the tree line. He walked out towards the foreigner and they met about twenty paces from the trees. The Inca turned and shouted towards the trees, gesturing forcefully, pointing from the young man's head held high on the sword tip back to the trees. He shouted some more, his words lost in the din of the battle, then pointed to the river, then to the trees, then drew his hand across his neck.

A pike was brought forth and the head placed upon it. The former Inca Administrator pushed the base of the pike into the soft ground of the field. As he leaned into it, his hands slipped on the blood draining down its length. He turned to the trees and pointed there again, then to the head, and then once again drew his hand across his neck, his now bloody fingers leaving a bright crimson line in their wake.

The advisor met the eyes of the King and pondered, "One must wonder what else we see that is not what we see."

The King's brow drew closed, and worry again flickered across his eyes.

A deafening chorus of screams arose from the ravine below the South. The pots of boiling oil had been lifted to the battlements and poured down on those below. Flaming arrows followed. Hundreds of Inca slaves died a horrible death at the base of the cliff, their writhing, burning bodies punctured by arrows rained down upon them.

The Inca arrows ceased rising from the ravine. The few remaining slaves in the ranks turned and ran away, mixed with the retreating handful of foreigners who commanded them. Only the archers remained disciplined, skillfully withdrawing from cover to cover, avoiding the arrows that chased them from above, punctuating their defeat.

A roar of triumph arose from the South. The King looked down to the Sacrificador command post. His son, beaming, gazed up at him. Their eyes met. Slowly, the Prince raised his right hand and clinched his fist. Then he yelled, "Victory! We are the Atacameños! None shall breach Pukara de Quitor!"

Chapter Two

The Prince was surrounded by his commanders, fists raised in triumph. They lifted him upon their shoulders, and began a long, snaking dance of victory through the fortress, climbing slowly up to the King.

The people of the fortress burst forth from their places of hiding and joined in the celebration. Shouts of jubilation filled the air.

"Victory! Triumph for the Atacameños!" the people cried. The masses joined the victory march of the Prince, still hoisted by his commanders.

Looking down from the royal terrace, the Queen joined the King and his advisor. They watched the victory procession climb the final steps to the peak.

"We have done well, my King," she observed softly, but with discernable pride.

The King replied as only a parent could, "It has not been without its struggles, but, yes, we have done well. He will be a fine King, a fine leader of his people."

With a final burst of shouts and accolades, the Prince and his commanders entered the royal terrace. The Prince, vibrant with the adrenaline of battle and the freedom of victory, approached the King and Queen.

The Prince dropped to one knee and proclaimed, "My Queen, my King, I bring you victory!" He looked up, unable to suppress his smile.

"Rise, my son!" commanded the King. "Join us here, show yourself to the people."

The Prince moved to their side and they turned to face the crowds below. They joined hands and raised them as one.

"My people!" shouted the King. "I give you victory! I give you your hero! I give you the Prince!"

The roar from the Atacameños people filled the entire valley, shook the walls, and rattled the trees where the remaining Incas shivered in fear.

The King soaked up the sound and cast his gaze wide across his dominion.

"All is well," he reflected, as much to himself as to the Queen and Prince. "The Condor brings the truth."

"The Condor brings the truth," he declared louder, then turned and repeated it to the rapidly filling royal terrace. "The Condor brings the truth!"

Chapter Two

"The Condor!" the people on the terrace proclaimed. Then they repeated it again, growing in volume, confidence and synchronization, "The Condor!"

The crowd below took up the chant, "The Condor! The Condor! The Condor!"

The commanders on the royal terrace swept forward, and again hoisted the Prince on their shoulders, leading the refrain, "The Condor! The Condor! The Condor!"

The King turned and kissed his wife, the Queen, the love in his heart glowing in his eyes. They began as a typical politically expedient match of Prince and Princess, much as their eldest daughter was entering tomorrow, but their marriage had grown into deep respect and abiding love.

The King saw their future in her eyes. It was a graceful final chapter, with their children fulfilling their destinies, and their son, the crown Prince, taking his place as the next name spoken.

The Queen returned his gaze in full, her dark eyes brimming with love and admiration, backed by the iron will and indomitable spirit that won his heart.

"My King," she vowed, "this is truly our greatest glory. Your name shall be spoken in reverence for centuries to come."

"Thank you, my Queen," he responded, "But, my glory means little compared to our child, our son, our Prince, speaking his own name after I am gone. That, and that alone, will be our greatest glory."

He saw that his words resonated in her heart. Her eyes grew moist.

"Yes, this is so, my King," she professed, using every ounce of her formidable strength to hold back her tears of joy. "It is my greatest happiness to see our children reach their destiny." She paused and looked into his eyes, then added with a hint of a wink and a wry smile, "And every little struggle along the way has been worth the result."

The King laughed out loud and kissed her again. The kiss was tender, lengthy, and filled with love.

They turned back to the fortress and joined in the chorus, "The Condor! The Condor! The Condor!"

Amidst the tumult on the terrace, the younger Princess searched each face, desperate to see the General of the North. Finally, across the full width of the terrace, she saw him enter, his taciturn face in stark contrast to the sea of levity before her.

She braved an open and brazen wave to him, judging it would not be noticed in the commotion, but he did not see her. His gaze was set to mid-distance, and he paid little attention to the people congratulating him on the victory of the day. He nodded to each, and with as much courtesy as possible, accepted their praise. He then quickly moved on, unwilling to engage anyone in meaningful conversation. He, too, was intent on reaching someone as he moved across the mob.

Finally, reaching the point she could stand it no longer, the younger Princess gave up her position among the royal family and charged out into the crowd. Her older sister snorted a rebuke and her younger brother called after her, but she did not look back. She brushed past those seeking to celebrate with her and ignored those wishing for her presence to elevate their status. She took the direct route when possible, and the path of least resistance when required, but nothing would stop her, nothing would stand in her way, as she formed a wake through the masses.

None of this escaped the sharp eye of the Queen, who nudged the King and, with a slight turn of her head, directed his gaze at the mighty force splitting the crush of bodies on the terrace.

"She has her mother's strength of purpose," the King observed dryly, a hint of humor glinting in his eyes.

The Queen elbowed him and added, "I think that today may finally be the day it is revealed."

The King raised his eyebrows in mock shock and replied, "What is this of which you speak? Are you saying our youngest daughter's heart is smitten?"

The Queen elbowed the King again, this time hard enough to count, and replied, "One cannot be both the wisest in the land at dawn and the dimmest in the land before noon, my King." She turned to him and smiled.

The King smiled back, and they both turned to watch as the younger Princess found her mark.

Splitting two junior commanders who had cornered the General of the North, she took her stance before him. Winded from the voyage through the sea of revelers, she panted out, "General, I come to offer my congratulations on your victory."

At the sound of her voice, his head raised, his eyes brightened, and the first smile of the day spread across his face. "Ttt...," he began, and then he caught himself, suddenly aware of the circle of courtiers and commanders watching this extraordinary scene. "My Princess," he stammered out, "I am honored by your presence, and your congratulations mean more to me than the victory."

Their eyes met, their cheeks flushed, and they knew that it was over; they would never be able to pretend again. A knowing murmur rolled around the rapt audience surrounding them. The secret was out; the long suspense ended, the rumors were true.

"Come," beckoned the younger Princess, "you must come and describe every detail of the battle to me. Let us retire to a place where I can hear you speak." With that, the Princess accepted his arm, and they turned toward the royal family, still standing in their places. This time, the Princess did not need to fight her way through the crowd. The news flashed like lightning through the assembled merrymakers, and the sea parted before them.

They made their way off the terrace to a side alcove, one with an expansive view of the river canyon to the North, bounded by its towering cliffs.

As soon as they turned the corner, the Princess fell into his arms, tears welling up in her eyes. "I was so worried for you," she choked out. "I feared I would never feel the security of your arms again."

"Oh, dear Two," he replied. "What have you to worry about? I was in no danger! A llama could be General of the North! Look at this before you! Could a man, any man, scale these vertical cliffs? The General of the North is a useless title given to the weakest and the least. I did nothing for this victory. I did nothing in this battle but watch the bravery and glory of my dearest friend. I am nothing. I am unworthy of your love. I am unworthy of you. I must leave you, now, and forever."

"No!" the Princess shouted. "You are as brave and strong as any of the others! You are more worthy than any!"

"Your words ring hollow, my Princess," the General replied coldly. "You would not need to reassure me if your words of praise were true. I spoke the truth. I am the least. I am nothing. I deserve nothing. I am unworthy of you."

With that, he turned on his heel and walked away.

The Princess leapt after him, pleading, "No, no, don't go, I love you!"

But, her words did not reach him; he was already engulfed by the noise of the royal terrace. He walked away, steadily away, and was swallowed by the ocean of celebrants.

The Princess collapsed in the alcove. Hot tears poured down her cheeks and sobs racked her body.

She cried there for an eternity, until her life was drained, until a soft hand touched her cheek. The younger Princess looked up and could not believe who came to offer her comfort.

It was her sister, the eldest Princess, the coldest, most heartless person in the entire realm, who had never had a kind word to say to her the younger Princess's entire life.

The eldest Princess lifted her gently, and then enveloped her in a warm, loving, caring embrace. She held her until the sobs subsided, petting her hair and whispering gentle comforts in her ear.

When the younger Princess had cried herself out, the eldest Princess tenderly put her back down on the alcove bench, and sat beside her.

"Little sister," she began, "I know your heart is broken. I know you have loved him since you were but a young girl. I know you waited for today for years and years, dreaming of it every night, longing for it with every sunrise."

"But, how, how could you know?" asked the younger Princess.

"Because I love you, and it was written in your eyes for all who love you to see," replied her older sister.

"But, why, why this love for me now, when you have never shown me any before?" asked the younger Princess, with a hint of suspicion tinged with long held resentment.

"Because, my dear sister, you are the only one of the two of us who has ever had a chance for love. I knew since my earliest years of life that I would be parceled out, traded, like a basket of maize, in the interest of a political relationship.

"I knew that I would never have the chance to feel love welling up in my chest until it burst my ribs, to be senseless in the fog of love, to have my entire world light up when my love walked in the room.

"I knew I was sentenced to a life of duty, to be married to whatever dolt happened to offer the best alliance for the kingdom.

"I knew that was my lot in life, and I accepted it. Although, yes, it is true, I did not always hide my resentment and jealousy of you for having the chance to love, to live love, to be love. I kept myself apart from you because every time I looked at you I was reminded of what could have been for me, and what would never be for me.

"It only got worse when you discovered your love for him. Then I could see what I could have been, right there, in front of my eyes. Your every breath was a reminder that I would never love, could never love."

"But sister," the younger Princess interrupted, "mother and father love, you can see it in their every glance, their every touch, even in their every argument. They were a political match, and they found love."

"Think of the names, little sister," replied the elder. "How many names found love in their arranged, political marriages? Twenty-five hundred years of names, and can you say one before our father who genuinely knew love?"

The younger Princess's blank expression told the answer.

"No, love is not my fate," the eldest Princess said stoically. "And, besides, look at my betrothed. Can you imagine anyone, ever, loving that? No, I will not know love. But you, sister, you already know love."

"I knew love!" wailed the younger, tears bursting forth once again. "My love has left me! My love says he is unworthy of me! I have lost my love!" The sobs returned and the eldest again held her until they subsided.

"No, no, no, little sister," comforted the elder. "Only his pride is unworthy of you. He is just a man, a man with wounded pride. He only needs to find a way to demonstrate his courage, his abilities, and his worthiness to his fellow men and, more importantly, to himself, and then he will return to you. His battle is not with you, dear sister; his battle is with his own self worth."

"Oh sister, if it were only so!" cried the younger. "He left me, he will never return."

"He will return, little one," assured the elder. "His love for you is as strong as yours for him. But, he must love you from strength, from a firm foundation of respect, respect from his peers and, above all, respect from himself. He will find a way to build that respect, and he will return."

"Sister, sister, how long must I wait? How long will I wait for my love?" begged the younger.

"An eternity, and yet, only a moment," counseled her sister. "Come now, we will retire to our rooms and make you presentable again. Tonight will be a celebration, tomorrow the festival of the southern sun, and my wedding day. You must be at your most radiant, your utmost beauty, and your most spectacular presence for these events."

Chapter Two

"But sister, will it be an eternity or a moment? What will be my wait?" pleaded the younger.

"Dear one, an eternity is just a series of moments. Take each one in turn. Your love will return," assured the elder.

Back on the platform, the King and Queen received the well wishers while exchanging knowing glances. They had many years of practice at small talk with others while communicating silently with each other.

During a brief interlude the King whispered, "What do you make of our eldest and her absence?"

The Queen replied, "I believe the day has had many surprises, with many more to come."

A roar went up from the people in the fortress below as another crock of chicha was opened.

The King glanced down and commented to his wife, "I hope they save some energy for tomorrow's wedding feast."

His wife smiled, her face alight, but as the King watched, he saw her eyes darken and her smile fade. He turned to find his closest advisor approaching, his countenance grim.

The King turned, and reading the urgency of the moment, demanded, "What, what is it? What brings such a serious face to the celebration of victory?"

The advisor replied sharply, "I do not believe this was victory. I believe this was deception. Look, my King, the forest walks!" The advisor pointed to the forest outside the eastern wall.

The King turned and studied the forest. Indeed, it appeared the forest was moving. It was moving slowly and steadily toward the eastern wall of the fortress.

"What, what is this?" the King queried as he squinted. "By the Gods, I would trade the high pastures for eyes that were half as sharp as my youth. All I can see is the forest moving! What is it? What is happening?"

"It is not the trees," the Queen replied, whose eyes were still somewhat sharp. "I cannot see precisely, but something is coming, and it is very large. Large enough for it to appear the forest walks."

"Get the Prince, now!" the King commanded an attendant.

On the far side of the terrace, the Prince was counseling his best friend, the General of the North.

"You are as worthy as any, my friend," the Prince reassured. "This battle was not as it seems, even now. The ranks were all peasants; they did not even know how to use their weapons. They were driven forward by the foreigners to their slaughter. If they tried to run, they were cut down by the foreigners' long blades; if they came forward, we took them with our arrows. It was easy, much easier than the earlier two battles with the foreigners.

"The only discipline and military skill exhibited by the Incas was by their archers. They hid behind their strange roofs with no buildings and only exposed themselves in order to concentrate fire on our warriors pushing off the ladders. Their archers were effective, and they killed many of our good men.

"This battle was as lucky for me as the last, when I was General of the West. Who could imagine that anything meaningful would occur with the General of the West during a battle? Would the cliff rise up and smite me? It was ridiculous to think that anything would happen there, as I watched that earlier battle rage and others earn their glory. It was pure fate then and it was pure fate today.

"Today's battle was simple. My father had the vision of where the attack would occur. We concentrated our defenses there. We expended almost everything we had in repelling the enemy. We prevailed. It was not any brilliance on my part, or my General of the South's part, or my commanders' part, regardless of what legends are being created at this very moment."

The Prince put his arm across the General of the North's shoulders.

"You could have done the same and would have done the same," the Prince declared. "You have always been the best of us all. All in the corps respect you. All know your talents. All know your abilities."

The Prince paused, and then smiled, beckoning, "Come now, cheer up and join the celebration. Your time will come."

The General of the North smiled softly and replied, "Thank you my friend. You have always been there for me, and I will stand by you forever. I will endeavor to earn the respect you have for me. Given the chance, I will show what I am made of."

"Good! That's the spirit! Now, let us celebrate! A cup, a cup for the General of the North!" the Prince cried out.

At that moment, the attendant arrived from the King. His countenance carried the seriousness of the summons. The Prince took one look and demanded, "Where is the King? Take me there, now!"

The Prince turned and ordered, "General, come! This is your time. This is your moment to earn your respect."

Within moments they stood next to the King, gazing down at the creeping forest.

"What is it my son? My eyes are clouded with age. What is moving?" the King asked.

"It is the roofs. It is the roofs and two huge lattice works, moving towards the eastern wall," replied the Prince.

"Now they are really coming," added the General of the North. "The battle of the South was merely a feint."

"What is our status?" the advisor asked the Prince.

"We have less than a third of our arrows left. We have water. But, these will be ineffective against the roofs. The only weapon that could stop them is oil, and we have almost no oil remaining," the Prince replied grimly.

"By the Gods!" the King cried in anguish. "I have been such a fool! They played me like a flute! They knew I would expend everything to defend the South!"

"Prince, can the East hold?" asked the advisor.

"Can it hold?" interjected the King. "The East is six men high and more than two men thick! It is impossible to breech the East! Of course it can hold!"

"Father, look towards the enemy and I will tell you what they bring to the East," the Prince interjected, stepping between them. "The enemy built giant lattice works in the groves, out of our sight. Their construction work at the base of the East in the last few days was undoubtedly to build foundations and supports for the lattice works. I believe they will place the lattice works upon the supports and thus create two ramps, at least five men wide, directly to the top of the East. These ramps will allow them to breech the East. Unless we prevent them from placing the lattice works, the East will not hold."

"The Gods, the Gods have cursed me for my arrogance!" the King cried. "I see the cost of my hubris. My kingdom pays the price!"

The King smashed his fist against his gold breast plate and gazed out on the steadily advancing enemy.

"A diversion!" he shouted. "A simple diversion to drain our resources, expend our energies, and give us false victory. I walked down the path like a llama led by the halter.

"They appealed to my fears, my prejudices, and my pride; and I willingly obliged. I gave them exactly what they hoped for, exactly what they needed."

He turned to his advisor, blood boiling in his face, his rage apparent, and blasted, "They are cunning, these foreigners. Much more cunning and devious than the first two times we faced them."

He spun back to the Prince and the General of the North and barked, "We must face cunning with cunning, match deceit with deceit."

The King smashed his hand into his fist and resolved, "We will prevail. We must prevail. My name will not be the last!"

No one spoke as they all watched the enemy steadily advance.

The King broke the silence. He turned his back on the battle and addressed the Prince, "Send a runner to the General of the East. Tell him we are aware of the situation and reinforcements are coming. Gather all available men from all fronts, and send them to the East. Their mission is to defend the East at all costs."

The King faced the General and ordered, "General of the North, gather your best men and defend the barricades. You must repel the enemy and divert them to the killing rooms. If you fail, the kingdom falls."

He turned back to the Prince and commanded, "Prince, take the Pumas and prepare the killing rooms; they are our last hope. You must provide the surprise that matches the enemy's treachery."

He held them both with his gaze and proclaimed, "Our main streets are barricaded, with our corridors open. If the East is breached, the enemy will find the barricades well defended and they will seek the easy path. When they do, they will have to fight us on our own terms, in our own defenses, step by step, level by level, bulwark by bulwark, passage by passage, killing room by killing room. We will lure them into our traps and slaughter them!"

The King looked the Prince and the General of the North in the eyes and told them, "There has never been a greater responsibility for any two Atacameños. The future of our fortress, of our people, of our kingdom, of our civilization, rests on your shoulders. Now, go!"

The two young warriors turned and pushed through the still celebrating crowds.

While shoulder to shoulder, shoving their way through the crowd, the General of the North complained to the Prince, "It is the same story. I am responsible for nothing. No enemy will attempt the barricades. Anyone with a brain will choose the open paths to the killing rooms and the labyrinth. Once again, I will stand by while you save the kingdom."

The Prince stopped and grabbed his friend by the arm, spinning him around. Through gritted teeth he snapped, "The time for self-pity is done. Your job is to defend the barricades. You heard the King. If the enemy overcomes the barricades, the Kingdom is doomed. You must succeed or we lose all. This is your mission, this is your duty, and this is your opportunity for glory."

The General of the North rose up in defense and then caught himself. He softened and replied, "Yes, you are right my friend. I am sorry. My mind and my heart are consumed by the need to earn someone's respect. It clouds my vision."

The Prince released his grip, lowered his voice and confided, "I know who this someone is, and have always known. She, her parents, and her siblings respect you more than you will ever know. I look forward to the day when you are more than my best friend, to when you are my brother too."

The two paused, and then held a long embrace.

"Brother!" the Prince breathed into the General's ear.

"Brother!" agreed the General of the North.

They turned and pushed their way out of the crowd, shouting for their seconds and commanders. By the time they reached the passage, the horns of battle were sounding, and the crowds were growing silent with fear and trepidation.

Three

The King turned to his advisor and asked, "What are our strengths?"

The advisor replied, "First, knowledge of the terrain of battle, which will be our corridors and defenses.

"Second, weapons optimized for that context: short blades, hatchets, nets, and hammers.

"Third, the defensive advantage, which requires a ratio of three attackers to one defender to overcome a well-defended position. Pukara de Quitor is so formidable, the required ratio is conservatively five to one.

"Fourth, the knowledge we are fighting for our kingdom, and for our lives."

The King pondered these for a moment, and then asked, "And what are our weaknesses?"

The advisor paused, and then responded, "First, our quivers are nearly empty. Without arrows we lose the advantage of the height of our defenses. We have no ability to fire down upon the attackers from the East or from the barricades.

"Second, our stores of oil are depleted. We have no ability to concentrate boiling oil onto the lattice works or into our pre-positioned corridor traps. We can use water, but thus lose the ability to follow the oil with fire.

"Third, we lost some very good warriors repelling the ladders to the South. The best men wished to prove their worth to the Prince, and many are now gone.

"Fourth, the warriors' spirits are low. They believed they achieved victory. They celebrated, they drank, they reveled and they relaxed. Their victory was snatched away and replaced by the prospect of bitter defeat. Now, they are called to once again scale the heights of emotion and exertion. It is a daunting task to relax and then build back up again to an emotional and physical peak. Of all of these, the last will be the most difficult to overcome.

The King looked back at the slowly advancing forest. It had almost reached the East.

"You speak wisely, my friend," the King replied. "Let us work to overcome these weaknesses. We cannot replace the lost warriors, but perhaps we can replace and rebuild the others."

He turned to the Queen, who had been listening closely to all that had passed.

"I am ready, my King," she stated, before he could even begin. "We will empty the royal stores of oil and gather it from every kitchen. We will bring it to the East."

The King's eyes brightened, and he responded, "Thank you, my Queen. Your mind runs ahead of us all, like so many times before."

"And, my King," she replied, looking directly into his eyes, "I will send the little Prince."

The King reached for her, and they embraced. He whispered in her ear, "Our sons will not pay the price for my weakness. I promise you."

She kissed his cheek and murmured, "We are your kingdom, my King. Your name will not be the last."

The Queen pulled away, turned, and summoned an attendant. She quickly passed the orders to gather the oil, and then turned to the little Prince, still standing at the ready in the royal positions.

"It is time for you, my son," she announced, her voice strong with emotion laced with steely resolve. "Go now, go to your King."

His eyes grew wide, then his voice burst forth, "Thank you, my Queen!"

He began to run, then realized where he was and slowed to an all but levitated walk, barely suppressing his excitement. He stopped before the King and looked up into his father's face.

"Little Prince," the King began, "how long have you been a Junior Warrior?"

"Five years!" replied the little Prince enthusiastically.

"Five years…" prompted the advisor.

"Umm, I mean, five years, my King." the little Prince said, deflated by his breach of protocol in not addressing the King by title.

"And, what did you learn about being a warrior during those five years?" the King quickly asked, attempting to prevent the little Prince from slipping into despondency over his gaffe.

"I learned how to find and carry water. I learned how to build shelter and survive in the deserts, in the dunes, in the salt, in the high pastures, in the cliffs, and in the mountains." The words spilled out of the little Prince like water over a mountain stream's waterfall, cascading and accelerating. "I learned how to read the stars, read trails, and how to find my way. I learned how to track and kill game. I learned how to heal my wounds and the wounds of others. I learned how to build my own weapons. And, I learned our warrior history, of all of our great battles and our greatest heroes."

"Who do you think is our greatest hero?" probed the King.

"My brother, the Prince!" the little Prince answered instantly, his chest rising with pride.

"What do you think makes him our greatest hero?" asked the King.

"He saved our kingdom! He foiled the foreigners' plot!" the little Prince replied, nearly bursting with pride over his brother's exploits.

"What elements are required of a warrior?" the King queried, his tone that of a schoolmaster, returning the little Prince to earth.

"Strength, courage, skills, and intelligence," the little Prince replied crisply.

"Does strength mean the warrior can lift a llama?" the King inquired.

"Oh, no," replied the little Prince earnestly. "Strength means the warrior must have a strong heart and a strong mind. The warrior who can lift a llama may not have the strength to endure when they are stranded, lost, and alone."

"Have you ever been stranded, lost, and alone?" asked the King.

"Yes," replied the little Prince, the memory flashing in his eyes. "On our moon watch, we were each left alone on the cliffs. We were each assigned a task to complete before morning. Mine was to retrieve falcon eggs for breakfast. I climbed the cliffs by moonlight searching for a nest. I was alone on a ledge when my foot slipped on a loose rock. I was alone, hanging by my fingers."

"Were you afraid?" the King probed.

"Yes, I was very afraid," the little Prince answered, his eyes still in his memory, alone on the cliff. "But, we were taught that all warriors are afraid, that a warrior who says they are not afraid is either lying or stupid, and neither can be trusted in battle. We learned that fear is normal, and you must turn your fear to your advantage; you must use it to give yourself strength."

"What did you learn from your moon watch?" the King asked.

"I learned to always test my footholds before applying my weight," replied the little Prince, his eyes returning to the moment.

"Anything else?" asked the King, knowingly.

"I learned that falcon eggs taste wonderful for breakfast after a night climbing the cliffs!" the little Prince beamed with pride.

The King smiled broadly, his eyes open wells of admiration and love for his son.

He turned to his advisor and asked, "Do you think he is ready?"

The advisor raised one eyebrow to the King, turned back to the little Prince, and asked, "Of the four elements required of a warrior—strength, courage, skills and intelligence—which one is the most important?"

The little Prince did not hesitate. "Intelligence," he replied. "Without intelligence to know how to apply strength, when to show courage, and how to use skills, all the other elements are useless. Only the intelligent warrior is an effective warrior."

The King heard the words as an echo. They were an echo of his own voice teaching his eldest son. They were an echo of the Prince, the founder and leader of the junior warriors. The little Prince had learned his lessons well.

The advisor turned back to the King and judged, "He is ready."

The King looked down on his youngest son and placed a hand on each of his shoulders.

"Little Prince," he stated, "today your kingdom needs you, and it needs the junior warriors.

"I want you to answer this question carefully and with thought," the King continued. "What are the junior warriors capable of doing in battle?"

The little Prince returned the gaze of his father, his brow furrowed in concentration.

After a moment, he replied earnestly, "My King, the junior warriors cannot kill a man. Unless we took him in his sleep, or with perfect surprise and perfect circumstances, we cannot kill a man. Our weapons are too small and our strength too little to kill a man in open battle. Killing is not the strength of the junior warriors.

"Our strengths are these. The junior warriors are stealthy; we can hide very well. We are small, so we can go places a grown warrior cannot. We are quick, and can dart among the rocks faster than an adult warrior. We explore, so we know secret places that only junior warriors can know. We have excellent eyes and ears, so we can see things and hear sounds that grownup warriors may not notice.

"Because we cannot kill, but can do these other things, I think the junior warriors are best as scouts, messengers, and sentries."

"You answer with wisdom beyond your years," replied the King.

"I ask you another question," the King continued, "and you need to answer with that most important attribute of a warrior, intelligence. You must not let sentiment or friendship cloud your judgment. How many junior warriors are capable of performing a very dangerous mission today?"

The little Prince paused. He counted the most able, and then counted again, eliminating his closest friends who were indeed his friends but not ready, not capable of such a mission in battle conditions.

"Five," replied the little Prince firmly.

"And, how will you deploy them?" asked the King.

"That will depend on the mission," immediately replied the little Prince.

"You are indeed ready," confirmed the King, revealing pride in his voice for the first time.

"Listen carefully, this is your mission. The fate of the kingdom depends upon your success," the King explained, the importance of the situation ringing in his every word.

In a few short moments, the little Prince learned the mission. His eyes widened at first, but soon narrowed, as he built his plan around the objective and the challenges.

The King finished addressing the little Prince, "Quickly gather your five. Tell no one of this mission."

Chapter Three

"Yes, my King," the little Prince replied, his heart racing. "We will not fail. Your name will not be the last!"

He rocked his right foot up on his toes and pivoted smartly on his left foot, just like the honor guard did, and marched across the terrace.

The King signaled his attending commander, never more than two strides away. The commander responded instantly. "Assign your second as liaison to my advisor," ordered the King. "We are going to the East."

The King then turned to his advisor and commanded, "Signal to maintain the balance of forces against the threat. Use all available reserves if necessary. I go to restore the spirits."

*****

The Prince and the Puma squad entered the dark room, the stark light of the doorway revealing nothing of the interior, their torches doing little more than flicker in the smothering darkness.

"Come, this way, the ladder is over here," directed the Prince.

"By the Gods!" exclaimed the squad leader. "This black cave of a room is infernal, I can't see a thing!"

The Prince led them to the northeast corner of the room, where a ladder finally emerged from the gloom.

"Follow me," he told them. "The trap door is directly above us."

He handed his torch off and climbed the ladder, using his shoulder and a solid grunt to force open the trap door in the ceiling, showering those below with dust and debris in the process. He scampered up and looked back down at the dust-covered squad, sputtering, coughing, and wiping the dust from their eyes.

"Behold the elite Pumas, best of the best of the Atacameños warriors!" he chided them, smiling.

They grinned sheepishly in response, and then followed him up the ladder.

When the full squad was assembled, the Prince opened the skylight shutters, washing the upper room in the harsh, unrelenting desert sun.

The squad looked around in bewilderment.

"A strange, intriguing mechanism the ancients built for us," the squad leader marveled. "Tell me Prince, does anyone even know if this system works? Has it ever been tested?"

Chapter Three

The Prince smiled, his cheeks blushed, and admitted, "Yes, it was tested. Once."

The Prince remembered the day from his childhood as if it was yesterday. His memories of the killing room came flooding back and filled his mind.

That morning, many years before, he and his best friend stole a llama from a farmer before dawn, using a muzzle to silence it. They wrapped its feet to quiet its gait across the stones of the fortress passages, and led it into the killing room. At first light, they opened the skylight shutters and then the portals. The llama stared at the west wall, moved toward it, bumped it, then turned around and around in the room, eyes wide with fear. The Prince and his best friend drew lots to see who would pull the lever and the Prince won.

The sound was like none they had ever heard, a terrible shriek followed by a boom. It was a boom louder than any in their childhoods, or in their entire lives. They were dazzled by the shock and terrified by the reality of their actions. Resetting was beyond their strength and out of the question, since the noise woke half the city.

By the time they scrambled down the ladder, the guards were sounding the alarm. They split up in the passageway, each sprinting towards their homes via the most secret paths of their youth.

His father's knock came early, before the Prince had even stopped breathing hard from running all the way back to his bedroom.

The questions were simple.

"Did you do it?" asked the King.

"Yes, father, I did it," the Prince admitted.

"Was anyone else there?" asked the King.

"No father, I did it alone," the Prince lied.

The consequences were brutal, but just.

"Then you alone shall learn the value of a llama to a farmer," declared the King.

"Put on these peasant clothes. Report to the farms, where you will find a small plot of land. The plot is the same size as the field of the farmer whose llama you killed. Build yourself a home. Plant, tend, and harvest your crops. Sell them to buy a baby llama. Raise it with care. Feed it your crops, and protect it from harm. If it survives, if it is strong and vital, when it is grown give it to the farmer from whom you stole. Give him the llama you raise, along with the allowance you would have collected in the meantime, which I will allocate. Go! Now! And, do not return until your task is complete."

And thus began a two-year penance for the Prince, exiled from the royal household. He lived in his peasant shack. His teachers came to him and tutored him alone. He learned how to plant and nurture his crops from the other farmers, who were kind to him despite his crime.

He suffered failures and small triumphs. He innovated ways to overcome his inexperience as a farmer by crafting daggers in the old way, chipping black obsidian down to a blade, grinding it to a razor sharp edge on a sharpening stone, and selling them in the market. He learned cooperation and competition in the marketplace, helping his fellow vendors to set up and take down their wares, and competing with them for the scarce commodities available in barter.

With his meager crops and his craftwork earnings, he finally saved enough to buy a baby llama. It died of lice fever the next month. He began again. His crops improved, and his reputation in the market grew as his daggers increased in quality and uniqueness. He bought another baby llama. This one survived, though only narrowly avoiding death when he overfed it. Eventually, it was mature, strong, and ready.

On that day, the day he knew the llama was ready, he led it to the farmer he had robbed. At the path leading to the farmer's hut he met his father, who was there waiting.

"How did you know I would be bringing this llama today?" he asked the King.

"Because a father always knows when his child is grown and has become an adult, just as you knew that today your llama had become an adult," the King replied. "Come, let us go and restore to the farmer what is his."

The old farmer greeted them with humility. It was the first time he had ever been this close to the King.

"My King," the old farmer groveled with trepidation, bowing. "Is there some problem? I have done my best to care for the llama the royal herdsmen loaned me."

"Rise, dear man," replied the King. "I am sure you have provided as well for it as the royal herdsmen. There is no problem. We come today to restore your loss. The Prince has something for you."

The King motioned the Prince forward.

"First, let me again apologize for the pain and suffering I caused you," began the Prince. "I bring you today a llama, to replace that which I stole from you."

"Your act is most honorable. I recognize your hard work and your carefree youth which you sacrificed to bring it to me. I thank you," the farmer responded, his eyes moist with tears of appreciation.

"It is I who thank you," replied the Prince. "Without your help and that of your neighbors, I would still be out there, killing crops with my stupidity. You all taught me much, much of life, much of what it means to be a person, much of what is really important, much that I will never forget."

The old farmer nodded, unable to speak.

"This, I bring to you," intoned the King. "It is the Prince's allotment that has accumulated during his service to repay his debt to you." The King held forth a bag of gold. It was more wealth than the farmer had earned in his entire lifetime.

"Dear King," the farmer stammered, looking up with reverence. "I am but a simple, old farmer. My wife was barren, so I have no sons to bequeath any wealth. Our needs are simple in the closing chapters of our lives. I ask you, let me keep just what little we need, and then, please, I beg you, distribute the rest to the needy, those with no good home, those with no llama, those with no wife or husband, those with no hope."

"You are a wise and generous soul," comforted the King. "It shall be so. Who do you wish to manage the distribution? Who shall choose the worthy?"

"I suggest the Prince, my King. He has lived among us these two years. He knows those who are pure of heart, those who are honest, and those who are truly in need," replied the old farmer with conviction.

"Then it shall be so," replied the King.

The King gave a portion of gold to the farmer, who protested that it was more than their needs, and handed the rest to the Prince for distribution to the poor.

When they reached the end of the path from the farmer's hut, the King turned to the Prince and announced, "This is the end of your path of childhood. You have learned the lessons required to become an adult and a true man. Your life is now your own, to live in the service of the kingdom and the people."

"It will be my honor and my duty," replied the Prince, unsure how to wear the new clothes of freedom.

Chapter Three

"And, it will be my honor to sit next to you at our table for dinner tonight," replied the King. "You have grown into a fine man, a credit to your kingdom and a treasure to your family."

The words rang in the Prince's ears, echoing up from the past.

The Prince felt a playful punch on his shoulder, left the old memories of his exile behind, and snapped back into the present moment.

"What, what did you say?" the prince asked.

"I said, I think I remember hearing something about that test!" repeated the squad leader, punching the Prince again in the shoulder. The squad laughed, all knowing the story in detail. It was one of the primary legends about the greatness of the Prince.

The Prince joined in the laughter, his blush fading.

"Come now, enough of old times," the Prince commanded. "Grease those pivots, inspect the ropes, let's get moving. There is much to do and little time to do it."

*****

The General of the North gathered his men at the first barricade.

"Warriors of the Atacameños!" he exclaimed. "No greater battle has ever been fought than you will fight today. Your bravery, your strength, your skills, and your intelligence will determine the fate of our people, our kingdom, and our civilization.

"If we fail today, not only our lives will be forfeit, but so the lives of our parents, our wives, and our children. They will spend their lives in slavery to the foreigners, just as the Incas you see before you.

"Our sisters and daughters will be raped, our Gods defiled, and our city destroyed. It is only us, this group of warriors, who can save our fortress, our families, and our kingdom.

"This group of warriors is made up of individuals, each of us with our own fears, weaknesses, and strengths. We must put away our fears, and use them to fuel our strength and our conviction. We must avoid our weaknesses and use the strengths of our fellow warriors to offset them. We must use our strengths to fight to victory! We are the Atacameños!"

"We are the Atacameños!" the warriors roared in response.

*****

Chapter Three

The King heard the refrain from the barricades as he ascended the East. The Atacameños warriors were pouring onto the ramparts from all parts of the fortress. As the warriors cleared the top of the stairs and saw the King standing there to greet them, they stopped, stunned by his presence.

The King grabbed each warrior by the shoulder or the arm and, with his iron grip, charged them for battle, "For your family!" to one, "For the Atacameños!" to another, "For the kingdom!" to yet another. He looked each directly in the eyes, infusing them with his spirit, and called those he recognized by name, asking after their families and reminding them of their lands or of some shared memory.

When the last man had ascended, the King walked with the General of the East to inspect and further inspire the warriors. As the few remaining quivers of new arrows arrived, the King commandeered them and worked the archers himself, passing out the arrows in ones and twos, each with an encouragement, each with a mission.

As he handed out the last arrow to an archer whose quiver held only two to begin with, he turned to the General of the East and promised, "If the Gods allow, I will deliver more of these to you soon."

*****

The little Prince's left foot slipped again. His hands, arms, and shoulders were burning with fire. He couldn't hold onto the rope much longer. He worked his toes into the crack one last time, pushing until he could feel the skin peel back. He tested the purchase and it held. He put a little more weight onto his foot, and it slipped again. Pebbles and rocks slid out of the crack and fell into the ravine below. He counted the moments until they hit and was not encouraged by the answer. He was still very, very high. If he fell now, the mission would be over and the kingdom would fall.

He wrapped his right leg around the rope to relieve some pressure on his arms. He took a moment's rest, then, using his right leg, he pushed himself over and swung to the left, working towards a wider place in the crack.

"Tooowheet wheet wheet," came the call from above. They were checking on him. It was the code for "Are you all right?"

"Not now!" he thought to himself. The last thing he needed was a distraction. "But," he reminded himself, "they are being disciplined. They are following the protocol. They are on the plan." They were the best of the junior warriors.

"Tweeuuu, tweeuuu, tweeuuu," he whistled back. It was the code for "I am all right, proceeding with the plan."

Chapter Three

His swing was a bit too short, but the strategy was working, he was getting close. With another push with his right leg, he swung left, pulled his left foot back and kicked at the cliff with all his might. The crunch of his foot jamming into the crack was nearly drowned out by the pain, but he could not make a sound, silence was imperative. He was climbing down into a battlefield.

He stopped to catch his breath and assess his route. He looked right to check the Inca sentry. The sentry was still oblivious, caught up in watching the movements at the base of the ravine.

He looked left and examined the cliff. One more drop down and he would be on the falcon route, the junior warriors' secret climbing path up the South.

He gripped the rope tighter with his right hand. He would need all its strength for this move. He counted the moments to time his breath, one more big breath in, and then he released the rope with his left hand and stretched left to full extension, putting nearly his entire body weight on his left foot, wedged in the crack.

His left fingers scraped the ledge, and slipped. He pushed up harder with his left leg. The upper crack edge encasing it ripped into the top of his left foot. He reached again, and this time his left fingers found a solid place on the small ledge. He gripped it tightly, pushed up with his left foot, released his initial grip, and found a natural handhold deeper in the rock.

He was at maximum vulnerability now, spread across the rock face. He was attached to the rock with his left hand and foot and to the rope with his right hand and foot, with no ability to go back, even if he wanted to.

At this position of full extension, his back sheath harness straps cut into his armpits, cutting off the circulation to his arms. This was the only position when the back sheath was a liability. Otherwise, it was completely stealthy. No one ever noticed it, even though he wore it every waking moment. Only his brother, who made the perfectly sized dagger and sheath especially for him, knew it existed. Slung between his shoulder blades it was perfectly concealed by his tunic and plates. It was an exact replica of his brother's, the only other one of its type in the kingdom. It was the little Prince's greatest treasure.

The little Prince shifted his weight onto his left hand and foot and swung his right leg in a tight circle to unwind the rope binding it. Once clear, his right foot dangled free as he grabbed the small ledge with his right hand, his fingers barely fitting next to his left. He felt for the crack with his right toes, searching for a place strong enough to hold and large enough for his foot. He was able to get most of his right toes into the space next to his left foot, still wedged in place.

Chapter Three

He reached out with his left hand and grabbed the handhold at the highest point of the falcon route. He was there!

"Tweeut, tweeut, tweeut," he whistled. It was the code for "I'm in, I'm on the route." The rope slithered back up the cliff.

He knew the topmost falcon route foot step was directly below the handhold. He pulled out his left foot to put it there, but nothing happened. His left foot was stuck firmly in the crack, wedged in tight. He pulled, and pulled again, but his foot would not budge.

"Swhaaat swhaaat swhaaat" came from above, the falcon's hunting call. It was the alarm, the sentry was coming.

The little Prince pressed his left cheek against the cliff and tried to melt into the rock face. He shifted his eyes to the right and saw the sentry picking his way through the rocks and over the bodies, making his way up the ravine. The sentry was concentrating on his path, not looking up at the cliff.

"I just might make it," the little Prince thought. "He has no reason to look up at this cliff. If he looks up, he will trip and fall. He won't look up."

At that very moment the sentry looked up. The little Prince could see the sentry's eyes. They were looking directly at him. The little Prince stopped breathing and waited.

"We will learn if the green-dwelling Inca's eyes can see the desert in the desert." the little Prince thought.

The Inca sentry stared at the cliff, looking for the falcon he heard calling only moments before. He knew falcons liked to nest and hunt in the cliffs, and was hoping for some eggs for lunch. He scanned the cliff for a nesting pair, and then turned to the sky to look for a falcon on the wing, but saw none. Disappointed, he returned to the path, walking his appointed route to the head of the ravine.

The little Prince saw the sentry stare right at him, look away across the cliff, look up to the sky and return to his rounds. When he saw the sentry return to the path, the little Prince let out a sigh. He snuck a look down at his dust-covered clothes, skin and sandals.

"If the Queen could only see me now," he thought. "What would she say to her youngest son rolling in the dirt like a llama until he was so covered with dust he blended completely with the cliff?"

*****

Chapter Three

The King looked out from the ramparts of the East to the approaching Inca slaves. Their ranks were hidden under the roofs with no buildings. All he could see was their bare feet, with only one or two pairs of sandals under each roof.

"The Prince was exactly right," thought the King.

The Inca's work against the East under the roofs had indeed been to build supports for the lattice works. And, the lattice works were indeed massive, consisting of wood lashed together to form a ramp at least five men wide. Once the ramps were installed and filled with Incas protected under their roofs, the breech of the East was certain.

Because they were so short of arrows, there was little the Atacameños archers could do to stop them. Each arrow shot now was one less available should the Incas ever be driven from beneath their protective roofs.

"What do you make of it?" the King asked the General of the East, who was positioned behind the ramparts. "Can we defend against this assault?"

The General replied, "It would be a waste of resources, my King. The roofs are impervious to arrows. Boiling water can turn the top layer to mud and delay them as it trickles down through the thatch and bamboo, but it will not stop them. Boiling oil could be lit from above with flaming arrows and could cause havoc. If we can set fire to the roofs, we may be able to force them to toss the roofs aside and expose themselves to our arrows. That would be our only chance, but we expended all our oil in the battle of the South."

"Perhaps not all," replied the King, spotting the Queen leading a column of women.

"My King!" she announced. "I bring you oil, every last drop in the fortress."

She swept her arm behind her, showcasing hundreds of women carrying jars of oil, small, medium, and large. In the rear, the cooking staff from the royal household followed, with giant oil vessels suspended on poles slung between them.

"Firemen! To your fires!" ordered the General of the East. The fire crews scurried to torch the fuel as the women poured their jars into the kettles.

"Prepare the lifts! Prepare to repel the Incas!" the General of the East roared.

The General of the East turned back to the King and remarked, "Now, if we only had some arrows."

Chapter Three

"How long can you hold without more arrows, General?" asked the King.

"Not long, my King, not long," the General assessed. "If we don't have more arrows, our efforts with the oil will largely go to waste. We will not be able to take advantage of our targets.

"The lattice works are too large and heavy to be pushed off by our warriors, and they would be cut down by the Inca archers if they tried. Our only hope is to douse the roofs with boiling oil, set fire to them, and drive the Incas out into the open.

"If I have arrows to take advantage of the targets, we can disrupt them. Without arrows, they will overrun us quickly. With arrows, we can hold them for a time and inflict many casualties. In either case, it will be up to the barricades, the killing rooms, and the labyrinth to stop them. The East will be breeched."

"I understand," replied the King. "When that time comes, fall back to the labyrinth and stop them there. Your courage will be sung for generations, General. Fight well, live long." They embraced and the King turned to go.

"My King," the General of the East interjected, giving pause to the King's exit. "These arrows you speak of, we need them desperately. Our ability to fight depends on their arrival. Who is it that may bring them to us?"

*****

The little Prince was cramping. He knew he could not hold on much longer. He tried again to wiggle his left foot free, but it would not budge. He could not move it. His foot was locked in place as if pegged there. He was using all of his strength, and it just was not enough.

His right hand began to slip from the ledge. He pushed off of his left foot and grabbed again. His left calf cramped, the pain unbearable.

"Strength, courage, skills, and intelligence; strength, courage, skills and intelligence; strength, courage, skills, and intelligence," the little Prince repeated in his head. The pain was searing, burning up his leg. His right hand slipped again. "And the most important of these is intelligence." The words came through the fog. "The most important of these is intelligence."

In a flash, he knew his only hope. He swung out with his right leg and kicked back hard, his right heel banging on his left. Nothing. Again he swung out and kicked back. This time a tiny nudge. His left hand slipped. With all his remaining strength, he swung out and kicked again. His left foot moved. The pain was overwhelming, his vision narrowed, darkness closing in. One last time, he swung out and kicked. His left foot swung free, bleeding steadily from the gash across its top.

He kicked his right foot into the crack and reached out with his left for the falcon route foot step. It was exactly where he remembered it. He reached left and grabbed the next handhold. He pulled his right foot out and moved it next to his left. He swung his left leg over and put his left foot in the next step. He was moving.

He and the other junior warriors carved these handholds and foot steps. He climbed this route repeatedly in the dark, by nothing but feel. He knew every one of them by heart.

He moved quickly now, scrambling across the cliff face, moving downward, ever downward, racing the sentry's return.

*****

"Now, open the light portals with the left rope, pull it down," ordered the Prince from below.

The shutters slid open and sunlight poured into the room. The smoke-blackened ceiling, slick floor, and three of the walls remained eerily empty, soaking up the light and returning nothing. But, the west wall illuminated and glowed.

The squad leader shouted, "By the Gods! It is amazing! It is incredible! It is bewitched! It is alive!"

"No, it is not alive, but we hope it is close enough," announced the booming baritone of the King from the doorway.

The squad leader and the Prince turned at once.

"My King! I meant no disrespect. It is so startling, so disorienting. It is like nothing I have ever seen," the squad leader apologized.

"My ancestors took no offense, squad leader, I assure you," the King replied.

He turned to the Prince and asked, with a sparkle in his eye, "And is it as impressive as the first time you and the General of the North saw it?"

"Yes, yes, it is…," began the Prince, his voice suddenly catching. "Wait, how did you know he was with me? I never told you that. I maintained my silence and deceit to this very day, much to my dishonor."

"There was dishonor in lying to me, Prince, that much is true, but you did it to protect your best friend. He was and is a worthy friend to you, to me, and to the kingdom," replied the King, placing his hand on his son's shoulder.

Chapter Three

"My King," the Prince admitted, downcast. "I have dishonored myself and my family by my dishonesty."

"Do not trouble yourself, Prince," the King continued. "I knew before you returned to your bed the two of you conspired to test this killing room. And, I knew of the help he and your younger sister provided you during your exile, despite my admonitions to the contrary. I made certain they were never caught in their efforts, and frankly, admired their courage in risking their own exile to help you in yours. As I mentioned, you have a fine and courageous friend as well as a strong and determined younger sister."

"You knew of the midnight cultivations?" the Prince asked incredulously.

"Oh, yes," chortled his father. "I even came to witness one. I nearly broke a rib suppressing my laughter while watching the three of you try to determine which plants were crops and which were weeds by the moonlight. If I recall correctly, you actually guessed right on eight of them."

The King's eyes were alight with humor. He and the Prince broke into guffaws of laughter at the memory.

"Father, my King, your heart is larger than your kingdom, your example taller than the mountains, your wisdom larger than the salts. Who could ever follow you?" asked the Prince.

"Only you, my Prince," the King replied. "I will be but a name, but you will be a legend."

The Prince blushed at the compliment, glancing at the squad leader, who was enthralled at the exchange.

"My King," the Prince replied. "We fight this battle today to preserve our kingdom and to continue the names, of which yours will always, for eternity, be the noblest and most honored."

"The King!" the Prince roared, stepping back.

"The King!" replied the Pumas, above and below.

The King looked at the Prince, then at the squad leader, and addressed them both, his voice rising up through the structure to the room above, where the Pumas stood transfixed.

"Warriors, these rooms were built by the ancients for this day," the King exhorted, his words echoing from the hard surfaces. "They knew if the unthinkable happened and the East was breeched, the fortress was at risk. These rooms have waited all these centuries for this moment. Use them well, use them rapidly, and use them relentlessly. Our future relies on you."

Through the doorway, they heard the horns from the East. The Queen appeared at the door, having witnessed it all from just outside in the passageway. The squad leader was now even more intimidated, the Prince more pleased.

"My Queen, it is my honor to be in your presence," the squad leader avowed.

"Puma, it is my honor today to be in yours, and those of your men," the Queen replied.

"My King," she announced. "The battle begins. We must go."

She turned to her son. The Prince came to her.

"Prince, even if I cast away all of my mother's pride, you are still the best of your generation," the Queen declared with admiration. "Today, the kingdom needs its best; it needs your best, if we are to survive. Give us your best," she directed, with an underlying current of love that was discernable.

"My Queen," the Prince replied. "It is with your strength I fight this battle. It is with your resolve we shall triumph."

Their hands touched, and they embraced. The Queen discretely brushed his cheek with a kiss on the lee side of the squad leader in order to protect his dignity. His eyes ignited and hers grew damp.

"My Queen," the King interrupted. "Come, we must go."

"Fight well, warriors, and live to fight another day!" charged the King, and he and the Queen swept out the doorway.

*****

The General of the North examined the positions above the third barricade.

"This can be improved," he told the squad leader. "Give me more overlap in the fields of fire and more protection from counter attack."

"It will be so, General," replied the warrior.

"You prepare well," the King commented.

Chapter Three

"My King!" the General responded, surprised at such a visit. Only then did he notice them both.

"My Queen," he continued. "You bless us with your presence."

"It is we who are blessed by your courage, strength, skills and intelligence," replied the Queen.

"You flatter me, my Queen," replied the General, embarrassed at such praise from royalty in front of his men.

"General, what are your plans for the fourth barricade?" asked the King, endeavoring to separate the General from his warriors.

The three of them turned and walked up the steep slope while the General described the details of his defense strategy. When they reached the top and were alone, the King turned to the General.

"General," the King interrupted, "your plans are above reproach. Your strategy is sound. Your tactics are flawless. I only see one weakness in your preparations."

The General of the North's face twisted, racked by doubts. His mind raced back over his plans. "What did I miss? What element do I lack?" he asked himself.

"My King," he replied, mustering all of his conviction and strength to maintain his composure. "What weakness remains? Please tell me so that I might correct it immediately. Retreat lanes? Fields of fire? Resupply? Please, let me address this weakness."

"General," the King began. "Earlier today I asked a junior warrior what the four requirements of a warrior were, and he correctly replied courage, strength, skills, and intelligence. He also knew the most important requirement, intelligence.

"I know, without doubt, that you possess all of the four requirements in great measure, as much or more than any warrior in the kingdom. But, I believe that the most important requirement, your intelligence, is compromised today. I believe you may strive too much to prove something already proven, and thus risk all."

The General's heart almost stopped. He was speechless and crestfallen.

"My King," he implored. "Please believe me when I tell you that I would never consciously or purposely compromise my performance in battle for any reason."

"General," the King replied. "I believe that to be true except in one case, and that one case is your love for my daughter."

The General nearly choked. His cheeks flushed. His embarrassment knew no bounds.

The General looked at the King and Queen. They were not angry, resentful or vengeful. They looked sanguine, content, yet concerned.

The King advised, "You do not need to perform heroic, mythical feats to earn the respect of your fellow warriors, the younger Princess or her family. If you seek to do so, you may make rash or precipitous decisions in the coming battle."

The King paused while the color drained from the General's face.

"He knows, they both know, they know all," the General thought to himself. "They've known all along, they know everything, even my deepest fears."

"We know about the two of you, and have seen our daughter's love for you for many years," the Queen added, echoing his thoughts. "General, it is of the utmost importance for you to know, right now, that given the choice of any man in any kingdom in the entire world, we would be honored to have you for a son."

"I, I, I don't know what to say," stammered the General, the hole in his heart ripped open for the world, and more importantly, the mother and father of the woman he loved, to see.

The King looked at the General and held his gaze, saying, "You will make life and death decisions today for yourself and for your men. You must make those decisions with a clear head and an untroubled heart. You must make the best decisions for you, for your warriors, for our daughter and for the kingdom."

The King placed his hand on the General's shoulder and commanded, "Go now, and fight with courage. Fight strong, fight skillfully, and most of all, fight intelligently. We know that this critical position for the defense of the kingdom, defending the barricades, is in the hands of the most capable leader in the kingdom—you."

The King and Queen then each embraced the General, silently passing on their confidence and their belief in him. Then they turned and walked up the hill to the royal quarters. The General stared after them, speechless.

Finally, he turned and looked out over the valley where he and his love walked for hours in the moonlight, the distant mountains topped with snow where they searched for wildflowers, the rich green fields of the oasis where they snuck out to aid the Prince, and the salts far to the south, where they traveled with the Queen to visit her tribe.

"I must see her again," he declared. "Whatever happens, I must see her again to tell her I love her."

*****

"Sister, sister, may I come in?" the elder Princess queried while simultaneously barging in. "Hello, are you well? Are you dressing for the celebration tonight?" The elder Princess pushed on into the room, past the attendants, into the inner chambers.

"Oh! By the Gods!" the elder exclaimed when she saw her little sister, "What possesses you? What on earth are you wearing? You should be in your party best. We will be celebrating the victory soon!"

"Dear sister," the younger replied. "Our victory is very much in doubt. This morning's battle was but a deception. The East may soon be breached. The destiny of the kingdom hangs in the balance."

"Pshaw," dismissed the elder. "We are the Atacameños. The Pukara de Quitor has never been breached. It will never be breached, certainly not by the East. And besides, no mob of smelly Incas and their heathen foreign masters is going to disrupt my wedding tomorrow. And, speaking of my wedding, have you seen the little Prince? I need him to try on his beautiful clothes and rehearse his part in the ceremony."

*****

The little Prince clamored across the cliff face, racing to get down and behind cover in the ravine before the sentry returned. He could hear the sentry coming, stumbling over the rocks and cursing when he stepped on a dead body. He was getting closer, just around the corner. It was going to be very, very close.

The little Prince closed his eyes. It was faster to climb by memory rather than sight. In his mind, he went back to his last night climb up and back down the falcon route on a moonless night. He knew exactly where he was, the next handhold was over and down—there. The next foot step was down—there. Four more to go.

The sentry's steps grew louder, his curses more intense, then—crack— with a noise that sounded as loud as a tree falling, he stepped on an arrow piercing a body. He was only paces away.

The little Prince reached down and left and grabbed the handhold. One more to go.

The sentry stopped, cursed, and kicked at the broken arrow.

Chapter Three

The little Prince stepped over, one last foot step, and then soundlessly lowered himself behind the boulder at the base of the falcon route. The sentry passed within two paces, now cursing even louder after scraping his shin on the arrow.

The little Prince stayed down and hidden until the sentry's steps faded. As soon as it was quiet, he gave the signal. "Tweeut, tweeut, tweeut," he whistled. "Tweeut, tweeut, tweeut," he whistled again. The rope came down the cliff and landed with a thud on the boulder next to him.

"Good aim," the little Prince thought. "Only a junior warrior could make that drop."

He picked up the end of the rope, ran out, and tied it to the top of an abandoned ladder lying among the crumpled bodies piled throughout the ravine. With all his strength he pulled four bodies off the ladder and dragged the bottom of it about five paces from the bottom of the cliff.

"Tweeut, tweeut, tweeut," he whistled again. "Tweeut, tweeut, tweeut," he repeated. The rope went taut, and then the ladder lurched up, stopped, and lurched up again. Again and again, the ladder lurched skyward, in a regular rhythm. The little Prince recognized the cadence.

"They are singing the afternoon march song," he thought, and began singing the lyrics silently to himself.

As the ladder continued its climb, the little Prince went to work, gathering his treasure.

*****

"We are ready," the Puma squad leader of the uppermost killing room reported. "All systems have been tested, and everything is functional."

"Have you picked a runner?" asked the Prince.

"Yes, he is the fastest of the Pumas," the squad leader replied.

"And, does he have the tunic?" the Prince asked.

"Yes, he has the tunic, and it matches the wall perfectly. It is truly astonishing," the squad leader responded, his voice filled with wonder.

"Did you test the door drop?" the Prince asked.

"Yes, and once we cleared and greased the track, it is working fine, just like everything else," the squad leader related. "And, if I may say so, my Prince, the ancients were an amazing people. Their brilliance makes me proud to be an Atacameños."

Chapter Three

"We fight for their legacy," replied the Prince. "We fight for their memory, we fight for their kingdom, and we fight for our future."

"For our future!" shouted the squad leader, and the other Pumas in the squad responded, "For our future!"

The Prince finished his inspection and climbed out the roof trapdoor to check on the battle.

The Prince looked down the steep hill at the barricades. The squads there were in position. He noted a new defensive position above the third barricade and instantly perceived the improved interlocking fields of fire. The Prince smiled.

"The General of the North has always been our best," he thought. "If only he could believe it himself."

The horns of the East were sounding the final call; the assault would begin soon.

He raised his gaze, saw the smoke from the roaring fires and smiled. He knew the Queen had worked another miracle. The East had oil.

*****

The General of the East grew concerned. The Inca ramps were nearly in place. He could do nothing more than harass them due to his shortage of arrows. The Incas were working essentially unbothered. His oil must be husbanded for the defining moment, when the assault began, or it would go to waste.

All he could do now was watch, wait, and worry about the arrows. "Where are the arrows?" he asked his second again, for the hundredth time.

*****

The little Prince grunted and tugged again. Finally, the arrow pulled free and he fell on his rear, almost impaling himself on the short blade of a fallen Inca warrior. The little Prince looked down at the dead Inca. The Inca looked different from the rest of the bodies.

It took the little Prince a few moments to put it together, but the warrior wore sandals, while the rest of the dead were barefoot. The warrior had a full battle tunic, a blade harness, and a very different face. The other dead were mitimaes, the slaves of the Incas. The little Prince had seen mitimaes before the collapse of the Inca Empire, when he visited his friend, the Inca Administrator's son, at their home in Catarpe.

Chapter Three

It was the slaves who did the building of the temples, the cities, the Inca road, and all the other major works of the Incas. It had always been the mitimae slaves who built and maintained the Inca Empire, and it had always been warriors like this one who kept them in line.

The little Prince looked down at the bodies and thought, "They were master and slave, but they are all dead together now."

He reached down and pulled another arrow.

*****

"Welcome King, it is good you returned in time for the party!" the Inca Administrator exclaimed, as if he were still an honored dinner guest at the fortress.

"By the Gods!" the King shouted. "Guards! Guards, seize him! Guards!"

"Oh, don't bother King, they are all, shall we say, somewhat indisposed at the bottom of the West," the Administrator stated with a fixed smile. "Those that remain are over here, with one of your little treasures."

The Administrator motioned to the side of the terrace, where three guards lay bound near the feet of his eldest daughter, seated in her royal chair, flanked by two Inca warriors.

The Next Name

Four

"Father, mother, rescue me! Get these smelly, awful men away from me!" the elder Princess screamed. She attempted to rise, but the two Inca warriors each put a hand on her shoulders and pushed her back into her seat.

"Do not worry. No harm will come to her if you comply with my wishes," the Inca Administrator interjected jovially. "She has been quite entertaining during your absence. However, I pity the unlucky Prince who draws her card."

"The rest of your children are being rounded up now by my men. So, in the meantime, please join me to watch the battle. It will be the show of a lifetime, which regretfully, in your case King, will be rather limited from this point forward."

The Administrator bowed low and swept his arm toward the royal thrones, facing out to the East.

Eight more Inca warriors stepped out onto the terrace to reinforce the invitation. The King and Queen, doing their best to recover their dignity, stepped forward and took their familiar places.

"What manner of treachery is this?" demanded the King, turning toward the Administrator. "Who has betrayed their kingdom?"

"Why King, you would have to ask whoever ordered all the warriors to the East," replied the Administrator, smiling serenely.

The King's face fell, and the Administrator read the story.

"So, you did not have to look far for who betrayed their kingdom, eh?" needled the Administrator. "I thought as much. No one overreacts like you, great King. You are very predictable."

"You despicable beast!" burst the Queen. "You ate at our table! You played with our children! You are nothing compared to the King! You disappeared from your post long before the foreigners arrived! You abandoned your people! You betrayed your empire! You are vermin! You are a sand beetle!"

"Now, now, my lady, don't distress your beautiful countenance," the Administrator counseled with a benign, tight smile. "Regardless of what you think of me now, I assure you I am much more agreeable than those who will soon be here. Things tend to degenerate so quickly when they join the party."

*****

The little Prince heard the rattling and creaking of the flimsy lashed-together ladder as the junior warriors climbed down.

All the while, he continued to pull arrows, counting the soft grunts as the others slid down the last section of the ladder and hit the ground.

With a quiet, low, brushing sound, as soft as a mouse sliding through grass, they signaled their arrival. The little Prince echoed the signal, giving his position. He hooted softly twice, signaling the position of the first pile of arrows he collected. One junior warrior headed there, filled his quivers and headed back up the ladder. The other three made their way to the little Prince, who was ready with another load.

Without a sound, one filled his quivers and headed up the ladder, which creaked and moaned under the load.

In soft whispers, the little Prince consulted with the remaining two, his two best junior warriors.

"How long for the sentry?" he asked urgently.

"He should be at the end of his cycle. If he sticks to the pattern, we have enough to time to get three more loads up the ladder," the oldest junior warrior replied.

"Then get to work. The East is doomed without these arrows," the little Prince replied, pulling another arrow.

The three of them spread out across the ravine, gathering loose arrows where they could and pulling them from bodies when required. Their steps were silent. They worked as ghosts, their dust-covered bodies blending with the ground and rocks of the ravine. Their presence was betrayed only by their shadows.

They worked quickly, and soon the two junior warriors had a full load, ready to ascend.

"Here, take my quivers up with you and lower me down another set," the little Prince ordered while handing over his allotment.

"But, you could be trapped by the sentry," they whispered in return. "We cannot risk the ladder. If he raises the alarm, you will be trapped."

"Enough!" the little Prince snapped, cutting them off. "Carry up my allotment and lower me down another set of quivers. The East will fall without arrows. Deliver these at once, and without fail."

"Yes, commander," the junior warriors answered, their eyes reflecting their fears. In turn, they each exchanged the secret junior warrior grip with the little Prince, then turned and made their way up the ladder, its squeaks of protest growing louder with every step.

The little Prince turned back to his work, picking and pulling, picking and pulling, harvesting the treasure of the dead.

*****

"Queen of the Atacameños, I must compliment you. Your efforts to gather oil were quite dramatic and heroic. You served your kingdom well on its last day. Those few who remain tomorrow will speak highly of you, I am sure," the Inca Administrator said dryly.

"How dare you call me Queen, you vile man," demanded the Queen.

"I shall use your full title until my associates arrive, dear Queen of the Atacameños. It will be your last chance to hear it in your lifetime, and I wish to give you as many opportunities as I can provide," he replied defensively, feigning offense.

"You are despicable. You are a traitor to your own people and a traitor to your former friends!" roared the King, rising to his wife's defense.

"Oh, now, King of the Atacameños, don't be offended. I know for certain you will only hear that title a few more times, and I will try to serve it up equally to you as to your bride, so that neither shall receive more than the other. All is equal in a marriage that smiles, yes?" replied the Administrator, his face fixed in an unwavering grin.

"This was hiding in the women's clothing," announced an Inca warrior, as he tossed the Altiplano Prince out onto the terrace.

"Oh, my betrothed!" screamed the elder Princess. "Have they harmed you? Are you still able to marry me tomorrow after we rid the kingdom of these brutes?"

The Altiplano Prince moaned and rolled over on his side, his high forehead bruised and his clothes torn asunder. He slowly rolled up onto his knees and struggled to stand. The King half rose to help him, offering his hand, but two Inca warriors stepped forward, separating them. The King shrank back into his throne.

The Administrator stood and helped the Altiplano Prince to his feet.

"Ah, the groom, I am so glad you have joined us. I apologize for the roughness of my warriors. They understand so little of protocol and the ways of the court. Come, sit with us and watch the coming performance," the Administrator invited in his most ingratiating and charming manner.

The Altiplano Prince, still dazed, groggily took a seat next to the elder Princess.

"Well, answer me, are you or are you not still able to marry me tomorrow?" demanded the elder Princess. "We have guests coming from all over the realm, special foods are being prepared, and performances by artists from as far as the sea, which cost my father a fortune, I might add. Not that it matters, since it is my wedding. But, this is important. Look at me when I am talking to you! Are you able to be married tomorrow? Well, don't answer me then, I will answer for you. Yes, you will be ready. My wedding is tomorrow, and no silly battle or invasion by these dreadful men and their horrible odor will change that. You must straighten up and get yourself together. You will be meeting important people tomorrow, and you must make a good impression. After all, you will be my husband. Are you listening to me? Prince, Prince of the Altiplano! Answer me!"

The Administrator looked at the King and gave him a bemused smile. He remarked, "Count your blessings King. You were lucky to be matched to such a formidable and capable bride. As I said earlier, I pity the Prince that drew your eldest Princess's card."

The King remained mute, still in shock over the turn of events. Then, he looked away from the elder Princess and the Altiplano Prince, and regarded the Administrator.

"How did you enter?" demanded the King. "How did you breech the defenses of the Pukara de Quitor?"

"Oh, it was quite easy, actually," replied the Administrator. "We came on the wings of the condor." He adopted a bemused smile.

Like a bolt of lightning, the truth hit the King.

"No one was there," the King whispered.

"Precisely," the Administrator replied. "The Prince was not there to perform any new miracles. In fact, no one was there, so we just came right in."

The King's mind raced. He counted twelve so far, and the Administrator mentioned more searching for the children. He guessed a raiding party of no more than twenty. If he could confirm the count and raise an alarm, they could still win the day.

"Such a long climb for so many men," the King replied evenly. "I salute your strength, if not your innovation."

"Oh, not so many men and not so long of a climb, dear King of the Atacameños. There, you see, I used your full title, so you lead the Queen, two to one," the Administrator replied, toying with the King. "You will not know our full number, and you will not be successful in raising an alarm. Can you not hear the din of the battle? You will never be heard above that noise, no matter how loud you scream. You are very predictable, dear King."

The King slumped into his throne, his mind alight, desperate for a solution, tumbling over the ever-changing landscape of the challenges, unable to get a move ahead of the Administrator in this game.

"And, besides," the Administrator added, "once my associates make their way up, the party will largely be over, so sit back and enjoy it while you can."

The King's mind seized upon that phrase, "my associates." The Administrator meant the foreigners. If the foreigners were coming on the wings of the condor, then they must pass through the ravine. He glanced down to the Sacrificador command post.

Only a few hours before, the Prince stood there in triumph, the vision of the future of the kingdom. Now, the King desperately searched for a sign of the junior warriors, hoping against hope that he would see no ladder against the battlements. But, there he saw it, the end of the ladder protruding half a man above the wall. The junior warrior sentry crouched beside it, peering over the battlement, moving his hand to his lips.

*****

The little Prince pulled another arrow, the last he could fit in his quivers. He turned and moved to the ladder in a low crouch. He looked up at the ladder. It was so high, it disappeared into the heights above.

He didn't hesitate at the daunting sight; instead, he immediately began his climb. With every step, the ladder creaked and protested. The rungs, haphazardly lashed, slipped under his weight on many steps.

"These ladders were not built to support men assaulting the South," the little Prince thought. "They are only props, as false as the morning's battle."

He was about a third of the way up when he heard the call.

"Swhaaat, swhaaat, swhaaat," the falcon's hunting call. It was the alarm. The sentry was coming. The little Prince had cut it too close; he was out of time. He climbed faster, higher and higher.

Then it came, "Swhaaat, swhaaat, swhaaat," a repeat. Something was wrong. It wasn't just the sentry; a double call meant danger. Danger meant there was more than the sentry coming.

He took another step, and the rung beneath his right foot broke. He slid down the ladder, and the next rung broke too, then another, and another and another. The sounds, as sharp as the flat side of a blade against a rock, echoed down the ravine. He slid faster. The ground rushed up.

He grasped the runners of the ladder as tightly as he could. The palms of his hands burned from the friction, the smell of the cooking flesh sickened him. Just when he thought he would never stop, he hit a solid rung and it arrested his fall.

He looked up. The next good rung was more than the height of two men above him. About a third of the ladder was below him.

"Swhaaat, swhaaat, swhaaat," and a pause, "Swhaaat, swhaaat, swhaaat." Danger. More than the sentry was coming his way, and whatever it was, it was coming fast.

"Strength, courage, skills, and intelligence; strength, courage, skills, and intelligence; strength, courage, skills, and intelligence," the little Prince heard the refrain in his head. Intelligence. He knew the most intelligent option.

He pursed his lips and sounded the call, "Suuueeeuuu, Suuueeeuuu, Suuueeeuuu," the distress call of the night bird. He only had to sound it once. They could not risk the ladder.

*****

The General of the foreigners looked up, hearing the sound of the birds. He missed the birds, the real birds, the birds of Spain. The damn birds here sang no familiar songs, made no familiar sounds. They were as insignificant and inferior as these pigs he had to work with and conquer.

He heard the call again and wondered what type of bird made that call, a hunter or the hunted. He decided it sounded like a hunter's call, a hunter like him, always hunting. For the bird, fresh warm meat. For the General, treasure, and of course, when it was there for the taking, fresh warm meat.

He walked on, stepping over the bodies when he could, pressing his boots into their faces when he couldn't. He hated their faces, their ugly foreheads, their dark skin, their coarse hair.

"Beasts, horrible beasts, that is what they are," he thought. He considered them gross, non-human, lower forms of life that he could not wait to be rid of, just as soon as he collected enough treasure to buy his future.

Chapter Four

Another call attracted his attention. It only came once, before he could look up, but it sounded very close, right up there on the cliff. He looked up and detected the motion. At first he thought the cliff was falling on him, but then realized it was only a ladder, an empty ladder. Then he saw it wasn't empty, and it was headed right for him.

*****

The lattice works were in place, and the Incas began their ascent up the ramps. The General of the East looked grimly down the line, the expressions of his commanders matching his own.

"Ready the oil!" he commanded, knowing that without arrows to leverage the small advantage the oil would bring, it was a pointless exercise.

The warriors heaved on the ropes and raised the kettles to the battlements, the oil still boiling inside.

"General! General! General of the East!" a small voice cried.

"By the Gods!" the General exclaimed. "What is a boy doing here, now?" he demanded of his second.

The second descended the stairs of the battlement and came sprinting back up.

"General! It is the arrows! The arrows have arrived!"

*****

"So you see, my dear Queen of the Atacameños, our lower average temperature allows us to grow superior crops, thus our foods are simply better. They are tastier, with more variety, and, if I may be so bold, better prepared. It is not the fault of your kingdom or your kitchens. You are handicapped with a burden that simply cannot be overcome," the Administrator goaded, smiling sweetly. "And please do note that you are now ahead of the King six full titles to four. I will endeavor to even things out before my usually dreadful associates arrive."

"You disgust me," the Queen replied, not deigning to look in his direction. "I would not eat your food if it was the last on earth."

"Oh, dear Queen, be careful what oaths you swear to," warned the Administrator, smiling. "You never know how things will turn out on a surprising day like today. Isn't that right King of the Atacameños?"

He glanced at the King, and then continued. "And, if you are keeping count, and I'm sure you are, you are now within one of your majestic and delightfully regal Queen."

"Oh, and look, the oil has been lifted!" the Administrator exclaimed. What a shame you used all of your arrows on the battle that was not a battle at the South. Now you will waste all of your Queen's remaining cooking oil, and your food will taste even worse than before. It is good that we won't be staying long and have to suffer it."

*****

The Prince stood on top of the uppermost killing room and watched the assault of the East. He saw the first oil kettles tilt and knew it had begun. It would not be long now.

He looked to his right and saw his best friend, the General of the North, standing on the defenses of the fourth barricade. The General returned his gaze; they held their right hands high, and then clenched their fists.

"To Victory!" shouted the Prince.

"To Victory!" returned the General.

The Prince lowered his hand and dropped down through the trap door.

"Get ready Pumas. It will not be long now," he ordered as he made his way through the upper room to the ladder for the killing room below. "Remove the ladder after me, and descend only for victory or death."

"Victory or death!" the Pumas repeated, as he disappeared into the trap door. When he hit the floor of the killing room, the ladder disappeared up through the hole, the trap door slammed shut, and the locking block slid home.

He turned to the runner in the dim light. It was uncanny; the runner looked exactly like the wall, like a living piece of the wall. The red of the tunic was an exact match.

"Do you know your role?" he asked the runner.

"Yes, my Prince, I shall not fail. I am the bringer of death," the runner replied.

"Your kingdom rides on your shoulders," the Prince replied. "Run strong, and run sure."

The Prince turned and left the killing room. He visited each Puma team in turn until the last, lowest room, where he stayed in the upper chamber, ready for the assault to begin.

*****

"We cannot find the younger Princess or the younger Prince," the Inca warriors reported to the Administrator.

Chapter Four

"Hmm, most troubling," the Administrator pondered. "You searched the bedchambers?"

"Yes," they replied, "and the entire royal quarters too."

"We found these in the young Princess's quarters," the guard reported, holding up her celebration clothes meant for that night's planned feast.

The King's eyes widened, then he quickly covered them, hoping the Administrator had not noticed his reaction. He smiled inwardly, his first since his return to the royal terrace. The younger Princess's ceremonial dagger he presented her on her debut was missing. It was a matched set. The halter was still attached to the clothes, but the sheath and dagger were gone. The young Princess was not just missing and not just hiding, she was hunting.

*****

"Make every arrow count!" commanded the General. "Wait until they flee the fire. Do not shoot until you have a clear target! The arrows in your quiver are your only friends. Use them wisely! Track your targets! No double shots!" Back and forth across the ramparts he walked, disregarding the ever-increasing barrage of arrows from the attacking Incas.

"The first oil is away, General," his second reported. The screams of the Inca front ranks suffering the boiling oil dripping through their melting roofs confirmed the report.

"Ready the flames!" commanded the General.

"Ready, ready, ready, ready," came the responses down the line.

"Fire!" shouted the General, and the flaming arrows arched down onto the roofs, which instantly ignited. Flame dripped down on those beneath, who screamed as they tossed the roofs aside.

"Archers, launch!" shouted the commanders, and arrows rained down on the ranks now revealed. They were decimated and crumpled onto the ramps. The next rank, its roof intact, walked over them, pressing forward to the wall of the East.

The General turned to his second and barked, "Pass the word to the commanders. Not so many arrows on each group. We shot three times more than needed. We don't have enough arrows for ten more roofs at this rate, and they have dozens."

"Yes, my General," the second responded, and moved down the battlements, crouched low to avoid the incoming arrows.

Chapter Four

"What is it?" asked the foreign warrior.

"I don't know, but it is as filthy as everything else in this God-forsaken hole. I cannot wait to get the treasure the Administrator promises and get out of here. These creatures disgust me," the General replied.

"Its eyes are open, but it is not moving. I think it is dead," the foreign warrior observed, bending down to look closer.

The little Prince tried to gasp but could not. He could not breathe. He was alive, but could not breathe. The foreigners hovered above him, their shadows moving, first obscuring the bright sun, and then uncovering it, making it impossible for his eyes to adjust to the changing light. He could not make out their faces in the alternating blasts of direct sunshine and dark shade.

"Look at all the arrows!" another foreign warrior remarked. "It must have been carrying 200 arrows."

The little Prince realized the dove had taken his breath. It happened twice before. The first was when he was very small and jumped from the low garden wall and landed on his back. The second time was when he was older, when he fell from the children's raven route, down low.

He pulled his feet towards his rear to raise his knees, then lifted his hips, lowered them back down, and did it again. Finally his breath returned.

"Ha! It lives!" cried the foreign warrior. "I think it is a young male, but it is very difficult to tell, he is so covered in dirt. Only his eyes are not brown with it."

"What cowards!" exclaimed the General. "They send their young boys out onto the battlefield to scrounge arrows. No wonder we conquer their empires with only a handful of real men."

"What should we do with it? Kill it?" asked the foreign warrior.

"No, bring it along for the Brutus," replied the General. "It's been a while since he finished off his last one. If we don't get him another one soon, we won't have any goats left."

The foreign warrior reached down and plucked the young Prince up to his feet, turned him towards the head of the ravine, and kicked him in the rear.

"March! March! You slime!" the foreign warrior shouted. "March to meet your Brutus!"

Chapter Four

The foreign warriors laughed heartily and headed up the ravine, picking their way through the bodies of the slaves.

*****

"I see arrows," stated the King.

The Administrator squinted and looked down the steep incline to the East. "My eyes are not what they once were, King of the Atacameños," he confided. "I believe I do see arrows from the ranks below coming in."

He turned to look at the King, eyes arched.

"You put much thought and effort into this attack. I commend you your forethought and execution," the King flattered him, hoping to trade compliments for more information.

"I thank you, King. Yes, it was much work and preparation. And, by the way, you are now tied with your Queen," the Administrator responded, turning back to the East.

"My eyes too, have faded," the King responded, hoping to keep the exchange alive, hoping to glean something new, something valuable, something he might use to the kingdom's advantage. "However, I believe I see arrows outbound, towards the lattice works."

"Lattice works?" the Administrator asked. "Ah, you mean our ramps! Yes, our ramps were also much work and preparation once we arrived. The planning was easy, as they are a small variation of what we use to build our majestic temples and towering cities. The engineering was trivial compared to those great works.

"It is a shame you turned down my invitations to journey north and see our cities in the sky, dear King," the Administrator chided. "Perhaps then you would have had more appreciation of who now opposes you."

The Administrator turned, smiled and looked back at the battle.

He continued. "Your world here is so small, so confined, so self-contained. It is no wonder you assumed that your fortress, so easily breeched by simple ideas, was impregnable.

"But, yes! I see the arrows of which you speak! Marvelous! You found some arrows! Well, this will extend our show. Perhaps there will still be some slaves coming over the wall when my associates arrive so they can share in the amusement. They do so enjoy butchery and death."

*****

"How many more?" asked the General.

Chapter Four

"We can stop no more than four, my General," his commander replied. "And they have at least twenty within sight."

"Then alert the barricades," the General of the East ordered. "Hold them as long as you can, then pull back. Your orders are a fighting retreat to the royal terrace."

"Yes, my General. We shall defend the royal terrace to the last man!" the commander vowed.

"Yes, to the last man," the General replied grimly, and turned away. The battle for the East, the East that would never be breeched, was over.

*****

From his position on the roof of the first killing room, the Prince saw the signal. The East was falling. He looked to his right and spotted the General of the North. They turned to each other and exchanged a simple nod. It had begun.

*****

The younger Princess felt her way down the passageway, unsure which way to turn. All the doors and shutters were closed. The passageways, usually so bright, open, welcoming and familiar, were dark and filled with foreboding. The people were gone, hiding in cellars and chests, praying for a quick end and a rapid victory. The young Princess did not share their hopes. She anticipated a quick end, but feared for the chances of a victory.

*****

The Inca slaves poured over the ramparts of the East, five abreast, blades drawn. The Atacameños archers fired their last volley and retreated down the stairs. The fatally wounded slaves fell inward, into Pukara de Quitor, the first enemy to ever breech the fortress walls, even in death.

Another wave came right behind them, pushing the wounded out of the way to their deaths far below. They turned left, then right, not sure of the way, but quickly saw the stairs, and then the ranks flowed down into the passageways of the fortress.

The ways to the left were tight, dark, and forbidding. The paths to the right were broad and open. The mass of slaves and the few Inca warriors with them turned as one to the right and headed up the steep slope. From the first barricade, the General of the North saw them coming.

He shouted to his men, "Hold as long as possible, but do not risk death here. Fight hard, but smart; save your arrows and your lives for the next barricades!"

Chapter Four

The screams of the approaching mob of slaves and Inca warriors drowned out his voice. They were coming, fast and hard.

The General of the North raised his hand and waited, waited, waited. It was critical that the enemy pass the first passage before they engaged. He waited until the slaves were three strides past the passage, then dropped his arm and screamed, "Archers!"

The arrows whistled through the air and found their marks with soft plunks, blood spattering the face of the barricade.

"Perhaps two steps past the passage instead of three, on the next barricade," he commented to his second, as they felt the bodies slam into outside of the barricade.

"Volley two!" the General yelled, and another whistling song told of death.

The slaves and scattered Inca warriors rushing into the wide passage saw the carnage at the barricades in front of them and sought shelter from the arrows' song. There was no way out to the left. A high wall lined the entire left side of the barricades, all the way to the top of the fortress. But, to the right a wide, open passageway beckoned, and they answered the call.

To the right they poured, down a passageway until it dead-ended, then left through a narrower route, only wide enough for three men. The narrow passageway opened into a broad avenue leading up the hill, all the way to the royal terrace.

They poured into the avenue, running for the open space opposite the entrance, when the first across bounced back into the following ranks. There was confusion as the back pressed forward, screaming for the open light, seeking the escape of the bright avenue ahead. When the passage was almost full, they heard a sliding sound and a loud thunk.

Those in the rear turned, and found the entranceway blocked. There was no way out, and the fallen in front blocked the way to the light ahead. Those in the rear screamed for the front ranks to clear the way, but each time the front ranks ran forward, they bounced back. Suddenly, the sunlight disappeared, the avenue disappeared and everything was black.

The lone Inca warrior in the room yelled a command, but it was lost as the floor tilted. The floor hinged on its southern end, dropped down on the northern end, and became a slide. The slide opened into the canyon, with the river far, far below. The now steeply inclined greased floor offered no traction, and the slick walls provided no handhold. The Incas all slid out, shrieking their last into the abyss, falling for many moments before crushing against the rocks at the base of the towering cliff.

The Puma team in the upper chamber pulled mightily to reset the floor, and then raised the entrance door, preparing to repeat the cycle.

"The ancients speak to you, Pumas!" the Prince yelled to the team. "They are proud of you today! You serve your kingdom well!"

The team turned from their stations to the Prince, a mixture of awe and amazement on their faces.

"My Prince," the squad leader exulted. "If I had not just seen it happen, I would not believe the tale. And what a tale it will be!"

"Your place in Atacameños history is assured!" exhorted the Prince.

"I am moving to the next killing room. Make sure to check the pivot wall after each cycle. We must ensure the enemy is routed up the chain, lest they spill over the barricades," the Prince shouted as he climbed out the roof trap door.

*****

Some of the enemy turned left when exiting the breech of the East and entered the labyrinth of the South. The narrow corridors were strategically blocked as high as the buildings, forcing all traffic through a puzzle palace maze, designed to confuse, delay, and direct the enemy to specific places.

The only exits from the dark maze of the corridors were welcoming rooms, lit brightly by torches. Their narrow entrances promised safety from the catacombs of the corridors. "Step in," they spoke. "Find solace inside."

But, when the enemy stepped inside, squeezing sideways through the narrow passage, they did not find solace; instead they found a mallet in their face, crushing their nose back into their brain, providing instant death.

The bodies were pulled in, stripped of weapons, and tossed down trap doors. They rolled down ramps into the ravine below to join the bodies from the morning's non-battle, which had been all too real for the slaves sacrificed to the deception.

*****

The younger Princess was lost. She did not know where she was or where she should turn to reach her goal. The dark, twisting, turning passageways of the labyrinth were doing their job of confusion, but on a friend, not a foe.

Chapter Four

She turned right, thinking that must be the way, when she heard the screams and roar of war approaching. There were shouts, commands, and acknowledgements from Atacameños warriors mixed with the incomprehensible babble of the mitimae slaves and the rare commands of the Inca warriors.

She turned left, and kept moving.

*****

The Prince dropped down into the upper chamber of the second killing room, only to be met by two knives to his throat.

"Excellent vigilance, Pumas," he congratulated them, pushing the blades back from his neck.

"My Prince!" the squad leader exclaimed. "We nearly slit you like a melon."

"It was my mistake," admitted the Prince. "I did not repeat the password, and you followed your orders. I will be more careful next time."

"How goes the cycle?" asked the Prince, rubbing his neck.

"We are nearing our maximum," replied the squad leader. "We are holding up well, but we will soon need to release the pivot wall and feed the overflow to the third room."

"Then do so, but signal them before you release," the Prince replied. "I will take to the roof and check the operation, then move on to number three."

The Prince climbed quickly to the roof and crawled to the southeast corner. The passageway running up the hill was blocked by a false wall at killing room two. The flow of enemy was now so great that the first two rooms were becoming overwhelmed, and some confused slaves, and especially suspicious Inca warriors, were turning away and attacking the barricades.

The first barricade was already breeched, and the second was under extreme pressure. As the Prince looked down, the false wall on the passageway up the hill pivoted open, and the Inca slaves surged up the hill. Forty paces ahead of them, a slave wearing a red tunic waved them ahead, then into the passageway to the third room.

The slaves ran after their compatriot. Except for the distinctive red of his tunic, he was dressed just like them. The red made him easy to see and follow, and the slaves eagerly followed the beacon leading them to safety. They rounded the corner where the steeply inclined passage up the fortress turned to the right. The slave in the red tunic motioned to them, drawing them into the narrower route that led to the bright, open avenue that climbed to the royal terrace.

They ran into the passageway, following the slave in the red tunic, who stopped in the avenue, his hand held high, motioning them forward. The front ranks ran to him, but suddenly bounced back. The following ranks flooded into the passageway, stumbling on the fallen until the passage was full. There was shouting and confusion, then a sliding sound, a thunk, and all was dark.

*****

The General of the North peeked his head over the second barricade. The immediate sound of spears slamming into the other side indicated that was not a wise idea.

"We've got to find a way to slow them down," he shouted to his second. "We cannot hold the barricades long enough to divert them to the killing rooms. At this rate, they will breech the fourth barricade and be at the royal terrace before the killing rooms finish them off."

The whistle of an arrow, the plunking sound of a ripe melon, and a slave falling from the top of the barricade into the space between them, splattering them with blood, drove home the General's point.

"Do you have any ideas?" asked the second, pushing the dead slave's bare feet away from the General's face.

"Not yet, but the challenge has my full attention at the moment!" exclaimed the General.

*****

The young Princess felt her way along the dark wall. She feared she was walking in circles and one more corner proved it. She had been regularly placing four pebbles together at the corners to mark her trail, and as she felt the ground at the corner she found four pebbles, carefully arranged in a square. She slumped down, frustrated, scared and tired, not sure what to try next.

She heard a loud clunk and voices through the wall next to her. She thought she recognized one of the voices. She turned and looked more closely at the wall. She smelled torches and saw light filtering through a gap in the masonry. She looked up and saw a shuttered window on the upper level, and knew where her only chance lay.

She sat down in the narrow passageway, with her back to the wall opposite, and her feet against the lighted room. She put her arms at her side, bent her elbows, pressed out with her legs, and then pushed down with the palms of her hands on the wall behind her back. When her arms extended, she pressed harder with her legs to lock her body in place, then moved one foot, then the other, up the wall. Bit by bit, she inched up the passageway.

She just cleared the last stone of the first level when she heard shouts down the passageway. There were people coming, and she could tell from the language they were not Atacameños. She looked down in the dim light as they entered the passageway. There were two slaves and an Inca warrior, who were as lost as she was, and they were frantically searching for a way out.

They stopped directly beneath her and engaged in an argument about the best option. The young Princess felt her palms growing wetter and slicker as she sweated out her fear. Her back began to slip and a bit of dust cascaded down the wall to the passage below.

The slaves were unwilling to follow the commands of the Inca warrior to advance. They ignored him and returned the way they came. As soon as their backs were turned, the warrior pulled his short blade and threw it expertly between the shoulder blades of the slave trailing down the corridor. The other slave turned, screamed with rage, and charged the Inca warrior.

The younger Princess's right foot slipped and another cascade of dust poured down the opposite wall, landing on the warrior just as the slave reached for his neck. The Inca warrior crooked his left arm, blocked the slave's arms upwards, and delivered his dagger underneath the slave's rib cage into his heart.

The Inca warrior wiped his dagger on the dead slave's tunic and stopped to examine the blade's edge in the murky light, running his finger along the blade to check for nicks from the ribs of his victim. The young Princess bit her lip, straining against the pain screaming through her body.

The Inca warrior sauntered down the path, pulled his short blade from the back of the second slave, sheathed it, and turned to continue in his chosen direction, around the corner of the lighted room.

The young Princess held her breath as he passed beneath her, not a man's height below. He turned the corner, and a moment later the younger Princess heard the same, strange thunk, and then another sound, more hollow.

She exhaled heavily, sucked in a deep breath, and continued her climb. In a few more moments she was next to the shuttered window on the second level.

She moved sideways until her right leg was on the window, reared back, and kicked against it. It did not yield. She kicked it again. This time it rattled. She kicked again, and again, each time the window becoming looser and looser. With one last, mighty kick, she stomped down on the window, but before her foot made contact, the shutter swung open. Her foot sailed unimpeded into the upper level, she lost her leverage against the wall, and fell down backward. The last thing she saw was an upside down image of the wall across from the lighted room.

*****

The floor of killing room three locked back into place. The portals opened, and the west wall glowed, alive with the scene of the open, inviting avenue up the fortress to the royal terrace. There was a soft click, the avenue opened, and out stepped the slave in the red tunic.

"Ready to cycle?" called down the Puma squad leader.

"Ready!" shouted the runner. "Check for my signal before you open the passage."

"Will do!" the squad leader confirmed.

And the cycle began again.

*****

The young Princess woke slowly, her head pounding.

"My Princess," the familiar voice asked. "What ever are you doing here? We almost killed you!"

"What happened? Where am I?" asked the young Princess, her mind foggy and unclear.

"You are in the labyrinth, in the second level of a catch chamber," the familiar voice replied. "You were kicking in the window to this room when my men caught your leg. They were sent up here to kill you, but ended up saving your life. You nearly fell to the passage below and would surely have been killed. As it was, you hit your head very hard on the wall outside. You were knocked senseless for some time."

"My Princess, what are you doing here?" the familiar voice asked again.

"I, I don't know. I can't remember. My head hurts so much. I know it was important. I know I was trying desperately to find something. It was to help someone, but I can't remember anything right now, except that I know you, I know your voice. Who are you?" the Princess asked.

"I am the General of the East, directing the labyrinth defenses of the royal terrace. I have known you since you were born. I taught you and your older brother how to throw a knife, much to the chagrin of your mother. Especially since you both passed the skill down to your younger brother, who is a better knifeman than either of you," the familiar voice replied.

"What is the battle, who is the enemy?" the younger Princess asked.

"The fortress has been breeched by the Incas, led by the foreigners," the General lamented. "They used an army of mitimae slaves as grist for our mill. They overwhelmed our defenses with numbers while holding back their elite warriors for the final battle."

"Incas, I know I saw Incas," the Princess moaned, still groggy.

"You must have witnessed the Inca killing the two slaves below you as you climbed. We eliminated him just before you began your kicking, and the slaves he killed were still gurgling when we pulled them from the passage. They were expertly sliced by an Inca blade. That must be your Inca," assured the General.

"It was Incas. My father and mother, and Incas," the young Princess murmured dreamily, slipping out of consciousness.

"Now, my dear, you sleep now, rest, give your head some rest," the General comforted.

The General looked at his strongest man and ordered, "You stay here and guard the Princess. Let no one in and no one out. It is your life if these orders are not obeyed."

"Yes, my General!" the warrior snapped, his hand on his blade, ready to defend the Princess at all costs. "No one in and no one out. Understood."

Five

The Prince peered over the edge of the roof of killing room four. The second barricade was nearly breeched, and the mass of slaves flowing up the hill from the East was undiminished.

He slumped back down to the roof, his back against the bulwark.

"They are flooding us with bodies!" he exclaimed to his second. "Even the most ingenious killing machines ever devised cannot kill enough, fast enough. Unless the barricades hold, they will overwhelm our defenses and reach the royal terrace."

"Is there any way to slow them at the barricades?" asked the second.

"Not that I can see," replied the Prince. "If anyone can think of a way, it is the General of the North. He is the best of us all."

The Prince crawled to the trap door, and they climbed down into the second level of killing room four.

The portals were open and the room was filling. From his position, the Prince could see straight down into the room, the bright sunshine blinded anyone looking up, so they could not see him from below.

He watched as they stumbled and tumbled into the room. It was almost full and ready to cycle. There were as many down as were up, their bare feet waving at the sky as they slid out into the canyon.

"Can you cycle any faster?" the Prince pressed the squad leader.

*****

The General of the North gave the signal to fall back; the second barricade was lost. As they took up their positions amongst the pre-positioned arrows, spears, and blades of the third barricade, the warriors exchanged glances. They were all well educated and could do the math. They saw that at this rate, they would run out of barricades before the Incas ran out of slaves.

"By the Gods! We've got to slow them down," the General cursed as he slid down next to his second.

Chapter Five

"Here, General, have some water, it will do you good," said the second, holding out a jar of cool water.

The General reached for the jar but it slipped from his hand, shattering on the ground into hundreds of pointed shards.

"Oh, my General, my apologies, it was my clumsiness," the second pleaded. "Here, take another."

The General did not take the second bottle. He looked down at the broken shards, remembering the slave's bare feet waving in the air between them only a short time before.

"Can we get some men to the pepper trees?" he asked his second.

"The pepper trees, General? Isn't this a bad time to be grinding flour?" the second asked.

"Not for the pods, you idiot, for the thorns!" shouted the General.

"Commander! Commander, get me all the men you can spare!" the General shouted.

*****

"We found him hiding in the flour bin," the Inca warrior spat out as he shoved the King's advisor forward.

The advisor stumbled, went down almost to one knee, and then righted himself, attempting dignity.

The advisor's hair stood out in all directions. He was white from head to toe. His eyes were two dark circles on a form as stark as the salt flats of the south.

"Ah, dear advisor, my, my, my, what an appearance. There was no need for such drastic measures; we would have found you anyway. We will find everyone anyway. Well, no matter, welcome to the performance," cooed the Administrator. "It is so good to see you again. Here, take this and wipe yourself off. How is your youngest son? He was always such a bright boy. I understand he is a General now. Is that so? He has achieved much success at such a young age. That is just wonderful, so wonderful. But, he was always the best and the brightest. 'The best of us all,' the Prince would always say of him. Come, come, and sit here, where you can admire the view."

The Administrator led the advisor to a seat facing the East.

"As you can see, advisor, the battle proceeds more or less according to plan," the Administrator observed with a touch of pride.

Chapter Five

"I assume *your* plan, Administrator," the advisor responded flatly, wiping flour from his face.

"Well, yes, as much as anyone's, perhaps even more than anyone's, my plan, yes," the Administrator admitted, letting a little more pride slip out as he gazed out over the battle. Dust rose, and screams and shouts boiled up from below.

"But, advisor," confided the Administrator, leaning down, "as you well know, and any competent General knows, no plan survives first contact with the enemy."

The Administrator smiled and straightened back up. He half turned to include the King and conceded, "You have revealed some things that were not part of my tours during my time here in the fortress. Those elements have required some alterations of the plan, but, fortunately, my commanders are flexible, can think creatively, and have the authorization to act independently in battle.

"We shall prevail. In fact, as I think the advisor here has already perceived, we are prevailing. The battle shall soon be over, and the entertainment will then be done. Well, at least, the entertainment that doesn't involve you, dear King."

*****

"Ah! The Brutus! I see you have successfully defended the base of the rope ladder," exclaimed the foreign General.

The foreign warrior at the ladder's base stood taller. It was the first positive thing the General had said to him since he finished off the General's cabin boy during the long ocean voyage to the New World.

"Yes, General!" he snapped out. "I have seen no local creatures. There has been no activity at the top of the wall. I have defended the ladder!"

"Well, that is good. I knew you would be the right man for this important duty," the General responded. The other foreign warriors struggled to hold back their laughter.

"As a reward," continued the General, "I brought you this." The General snapped his fingers and the little Prince was jerked out from behind the group and shoved forward.

The eyes of the Brutus grew wide. His mouth opened.

"Oh, my General, it is wonderful!" the Brutus exclaimed. "I shall, I shall, I shall, do with it..."

"For now, Brutus, you will do nothing with it!" the General shouted, drawing his dagger and pressing it into the chin of the Brutus.

The General turned and wiped his finger across the little Prince's cheek, revealing skin and leaving a long scratch that trickled blood.

The Brutus licked his lips at the sight of the little Prince's blood.

The General slapped the Brutus, then stood no more than a hand from his face and screamed at him. "Do you see that mark? If you touch it you will leave a mark! If there is a single mark upon it before I send for you, I will gut you! Your job now is to guard this ladder! Do you understand?"

The Brutus rubbed his cheek, glanced at the other warriors and looked back at the General.

"Yes, yes, General. I understand. I will guard the ladder until you send for me. Yes, General," the Brutus stammered.

"Good. That is good. I do not want to kill my goatherd for no reason beyond one of these filthy creatures," the General snarled.

The Brutus nodded, and then looked down at his feet, realizing that his demotion to goatherd was still in effect.

"Come, up the ladder," the General commanded the other foreign warriors. "Let us complete the conquest of this insignificant speck of a kingdom. Two at a time, warriors, two at a time, the ladder will not hold more. Hurry now! I want to be done before dinner."

*****

The younger Princess awoke with a start, her eyes popping open. She sat up and looked around. She did not recognize the dim room. She did not recognize the warrior standing guard beside the door.

"Where am I?" she asked. "What am I doing here? Who are you?"

"You are in the labyrinth, my Princess," replied the warrior. "You came here through the window. You were trying to kick it in. Do you remember?"

The younger Princess looked at him quizzically, her eyes squinting in concentration.

"Labyrinth? Through the window?" she asked.

Then it began to return. She retraced her recent past. Kicking the window. The inverted view of the building. The Inca warrior below murdering the two slaves. The climb up the narrow passageway. The trip into the Labyrinth. The flight from the royal quarters via her childhood escape route—that secret path she used so many times to sneak out for adventures with her brother and the General of the North.

And the Incas! The Incas! They were in the royal quarters! She must find her brother! She must warn him! They must rescue the King and Queen!

"The Incas!" the younger Princess shouted. "The Incas are in the royal quarters! I must find my brother! Where is my brother, the Prince?"

"My Princess, you hit your head very hard when you fell. The only Inca was the one you saw in the passageway. Please, lie back down and rest, you will feel better soon," the warrior reassured her.

"The General! I remember the General of the East is here! I must see him! I must see him now!" demanded the younger Princess.

The warrior's face tightened. Disturbing the General with this matter again could only bring trouble. His alternatives were bleak: defy the royal Princess or face the wrath of the General. He chose the lesser of the two potential vessels of ire.

The warrior cracked the door and shouted down the stairs, "General, you'd better come up here. The Princess is awake and is demanding to see you."

The warrior heard the muttered anger of the General building as he ascended the stairs.

"This is not going to be pretty," the warrior thought to himself.

The General brusquely shoved open the door, shot a glare that would boil water at the warrior, and turned to the Princess. His expression softened.

"My Princess," the General began, "it is so good to see you awake. How is your head feeling? Any better?"

"General," the Princess replied, "my head is fine, but my heart is sick! There are Incas in the royal household. I saw them with my own eyes before I escaped and came here. I must find my brother! Where is he? We must save the King and Queen!"

"Now, now, my dear," the General soothed. "You took a mighty fall against the building. Your head is still oozing blood. You witnessed a savage killing by an Inca warrior and I'm sure that made a large impression on you. There are no Incas in the royal household. That would be quite impossible. The barricades are holding, and none have survived the labyrinth."

"General!" the younger Princess implored, "I am telling you I saw them with my own eyes!"

"My Princess," the General reasoned, gently touching her arm. "How did they get there? If they did not come via the barricades or the labyrinth, then how did they get there? By the path of the falcon? By the path of the condor? By the path of the Gods? No human can ascend those routes. The only human route is the East, and to ascend to the royal household from the East, the Incas would have to either pass the barricades or survive the labyrinth. They have done neither. There are no Incas in the royal household, my dear. It was all just a bad dream. Now, please, lie down and rest. When the battle is over, we will return you safely to your royal quarters."

The General gently pushed her back down, smoothed her hair and ignored her protests.

He stood, turned to the guard, and leaned in beside him.

"If I am bothered by this matter again, I will hold you personally responsible!" he hissed into the warrior's ear. "Do I make myself clear?"

"Yes, yes, my General," the guard whispered. "You make yourself perfectly clear."

The General turned to leave, paused in the doorway, spun around, and looked at the guard.

"No one in and no one out!" the General ordered.

"Yes, my General," replied the guard, snapping to attention. "No one in and no one out!"

*****

"Throw them over! Throw them over!" shouted the General of the North.

The warriors threw the pepper tree branches studded with long needle-sharp thorns over the barricade. The effects were immediate. Cries of anguish and pain ascended from the slaves on the other side.

"Now, the salt jars! Toss them over! Bring more thorns for here, prepare the ground for them! It will flow with the blood of their feet!" shouted the General of the North.

*****

"So, as you can clearly see, dear advisor, we choked your defenses with the lives of the slaves, and now our best Inca warriors are surmounting the East. We will now bring the crushing weight of trained, effective, and efficient Inca warriors against the remnants of your defenses," the Administrator intoned as he pointed to the hoards of Inca warriors flooding over the East.

The advisor rose, turned to the Administrator and admitted, "You have made your point."

The advisor continued, as one responsible leader to another. "When you arrived with the Incas, we formed a mutually profitable relationship that was good for all kingdoms as well as the Inca Empire. Transportation routes improved. More markets were available for food and fabricated goods. Trade expanded. Life improved for all. It can be the same again. What form, manner, and amount of tribute do the foreigners demand?"

"Oh, my dear advisor, if only it were so," replied the Administrator, with genuine sadness in his voice. "These foreigners are not men as you and I are men. They are not builders of kingdoms, empires, and civilizations as you and I are builders.

"They do not come to build. They come to destroy. They do not come for trade. They come to rape, plunder, and murder.

"They know no honor. They know no common dignity. They know no morals. They know no respect for human life.

"They know no Gods as we know the Gods. The only time they invoke their God is when they curse or when they kill.

"They fancy themselves conquerors. But, in reality, they are but common thieves, rapists, and murderers.

"They do not seek tribute, a mere portion of the wealth and production of kingdoms; they seek it all—all the treasure, all the wealth, all the virgins and all the lives."

"If this is true, then you are as doomed as we are," replied the advisor.

The Administrator paused, then replied, "Perhaps, perhaps not, dear advisor. We shall see what this day of surprises brings. The condor has yet to return to his nest." He returned his gaze to the battle raging below.

*****

The Brutus looked up to the top of the ladder. His neck ached from checking it again and again since he arrived. Finally, after an eternity, the last of the other foreign warriors went over the top, waved back down, and disappeared.

The Brutus gave a half wave up in return to the empty wall, turned, and a wide, sloppy smile formed. He licked his lips again.

Chapter Five

He walked slowly over to where the little Prince stood, and then circled him twice, softly moaning and grunting. He stopped in front of the Prince and bent down, his face less than a hand away. His breath came in puffs and pants, and was so putrid the little Prince almost vomited.

The Brutus bent down and his forehead nearly touched the little Prince's hands, bound together and hanging loosely near his waist.

The Brutus stood and rubbed his crotch, his moans growing louder. Suddenly the Brutus let out a huge laugh, his mouth open wide. He hopped up and turned in circles, laughing in a broken, sing song cadence, his body armor shining in the sun, his helmet cocked back.

He stopped about three paces away and turned to the little Prince. He laughed again, long and hard, his head tilted back, his mouth open wide.

In one quick, smooth motion the little Prince put his hands over his head, reached down his back, and whipped forward.

The blade flew straight and flat, with no rotation. It entered the Brutus's mouth, pierced the back of his throat, and sliced his spinal cord. He was dead before he crumpled to the ground.

The little Prince walked over to the body. The Brutus's empty eyes stared up into the blank, blue sky. The little Prince reached down and pulled on his blade. Only the grip and the broken base came out.

"That is the trouble with these traditional obsidian blades," he thought. "They are sharp as a razor, but very brittle."

He pulled the Brutus's sword and used it to cut his bindings. He tried to slip it into his belt, but it was much too long and heavy. He put both hands around the sword's grip, raised them above his head, and drove the sword into the ground at the Brutus's crotch.

"For the others!" he spat, looking down.

The little Prince turned and sprinted to the rope ladder. He scampered up at lightning speed, ignoring the pain from his burnt palms. The rope ladder swayed back and forth, almost knocking into the column of lashed-together bamboo with a tree root tied to the top, the root hooked over the top of the wall.

*****

The younger Princess stared at the ceiling and formulated her plan. She sat up and looked the room over carefully by the light of the flickering oil lamp. It would work.

Chapter Five

She rolled to her side and pleaded to the guard, "I am terribly cold, could you please give me another blanket?"

The guard looked around the room. There was not another blanket to be seen.

"My Princess," replied the guard. "There are no more here to be had."

"Then take yourself downstairs and fetch me one!" the little Princess demanded imperiously, in the best imitation of her older sister she could muster.

The guard was taken aback. He had never heard of the younger Princess acting in this way.

"It must be the blow to the head," he thought. But, he had no other choice.

"Yes, my Princess," he replied. The guard listened at the door to be sure the room below was clear, opened it, and disappeared.

The Princess sprang up and tied a knot in one end of her blanket. She pulled open the right shutter, laid the blanket over the sill as close to the right hinges as she could, then jammed the shutter closed below the knot, trapping the knot in the room with the blanket dangling outside the window. She looked out, and by the light of the open window saw that the end of the blanket hung at least a man high above the passageway below.

"It will have to do," she thought.

She pulled open the left shutter and climbed out.

*****

The lead commander of the main Inca warrior forces surveyed the battle. The slaves were bottled up in the barricades, not making any progress after their initial success. Those who chose the open and direct routes along the right side were advancing up the hill easily, but not reappearing once they turned into the side passages to the right. As he watched, yet another group disappeared.

"I must investigate this myself," he thought, and then his eyes narrowed. The wall that blocked the advance up the steep grade for the last group of slaves moved away, revealing a section of open passageway up the hill. Standing at the top of that passageway was a slave wearing a red tunic. The slave was dressed exactly like the one who beckoned the last group of slaves down a side passage.

Chapter Five

As the commander watched, the slave in the red tunic waved another group of slaves forward and around the corner down his side passage. They never reappeared further up the hill. Something was happening to them. They were being captured or killed. Whichever it was, the commander was determined that whatever was happening to the slaves would not happen to his Inca warriors.

The Inca commander turned to his second and said, "The men wearing the red tunics are the key. They are leading our slaves away. Get me three squads of archers, now!"

*****

The little Prince peered over the edge of the West. The Inca warrior sentry was almost at the end of his circuit at the southwest corner. The little Prince had to act now or risk another pass by the sentry past the rope ladder.

He crossed the battlement, ran three paces to his left, and climbed into the water basin, which was three quarters full, as always. He silently lowered himself into the crystal clear water, squatted down, and fished around on the bottom for the breathing tube. His lungs were beginning to burst when he finally found it. He put the tube to his lips and raised it slowly along the edge of the basin until it was above the water. He gently pushed the water out of the tube with his breath, so it spilled over the end of the tube like a slow fountain.

The last little bit was the challenge. Clearing the last of the water without splattering it onto the battlement, or making enough noise to attract the guard, was always the hardest part. His lungs were so desperate he pushed the air out too fast, some water popped out of the tube, and it plopped back into the basin.

The little Prince pulled in a lungful of air, and then sat as still as possible. He was very disappointed in himself.

"How many times have I done this silently?" he berated himself.

"I invented this junior warrior exercise myself. I was the one who always made sure the basin was three quarters full, just enough to hold a junior warrior and the remaining water without spilling. I was the one who checked for the breathing tube. I was the one who taught the technique. But, now, with the kingdom at risk, I slurped out water like a new recruit!" he shouted at himself.

The little Prince stopped and took a deep breath.

Chapter Five

"I must put this failure behind me and not let it consume me," he thought. "This is a test of strength, of mental strength. My thoughts must be to the future, not the past."

He took another quiet breath and waited. He could not hear well through the water, but he knew from many missions to the basin that the vibrations of the sentry's feet were easily detected four paces away.

The little Prince felt the first vibration, then the second, then the third. He held his breath. The sentry's steps were coming quickly, more quickly than they should.

*****

The younger Princess pulled up with her arms while pushing off with her right foot on the window capstone.

Through the open left shutter, she heard the guard approaching the room, already speaking to her.

She rocked over the edge onto her waist, pushed up with her arms, and rolled onto her side, breathing heavily from the exertion.

"My Princess, I cannot find another blanket in this empty house, but we gathered our cloaks and…" the guard's voice trailed off as he opened the door, saw the emptiness and the knotted blanket.

"General! General! She has escaped! The Princess has climbed out the window!" he shouted.

The younger Princess heard the General pounding up the stairs, shouting oaths.

The door slammed open, banging off the wall. The General's steps echoed down the narrow, dark passageway as he stomped his way to the window. He looked down at the blanket, still swinging back and forth.

"By the Gods!" screamed the General. "To the labyrinth! We must find her before the main Inca force arrives!"

The General turned to the guard, rage boiling in voice, and seethed, "And you shall lead the way!"

The General shoved the guard down the stairs, their steps and voices fading as the squad spilled out into the labyrinth.

"I am sorry, my General," whispered the younger Princess, staring up into the clear, blue sky through her tears. "You were always my favorite uncle. But, I must find my brother. We must save the King and Queen. Nothing, even you, is more important than that."

She rolled over and crouched on the balls of her feet, hands down, at the ready. She looked out across the rooftops towards the North.

The flat rooftops of the fortress were cross-hatched by the temporary covers made with layers of bamboo, thatch and mud that shaded the passageways of the labyrinth. The covers, built while the Incas prepared their lattice works, had done their job of blocking out the sunlight. The labyrinth below was nearly black, almost completely devoid of light.

"What a beautiful maze my people created," the young Princess thought. "The ancients who created these plans were wise, and the parents of my generation who implemented them were diligent."

"We must not let this pass!" she declared. "We must continue the names!"

She looked again to the North. Now she knew how to find her brother.

"He will know," she thought. "He will always know where his best friend is."

She scanned the high walls of the West at the top of the fortress and spotted the Inca sentries. She looked down and cursed her choice of disguise.

"This red tunic will be easily spotted," she thought. "But I have no other choice now."

*****

The Inca sentry strode up to the water basin. He was sure he heard a sound, a water sound. He looked down and drew back. The water was covered with a thick film of dirty scum.

"How disgusting!" he exclaimed. "We would not water our llamas with such water! And the Atacameños drink this!"

He turned on his heel, muttering, and continued his circuit.

The little Prince waited until the vibrations died out. He knew the count and the distance required. As soon as the sentry was clear, he slowly rose up until he could see over the basin's edge and confirm the sentry was gone. He turned to check behind, and then climbed out onto the inner wall, being careful to keep the water dripping from him behind the edge of the battlements.

Chapter Five

He knew the deployment for battle. He knew who he must find. He knew where he must go—to the North.

The Next Name

Six

"Administrator! Administrator!" the voice called.

All on the royal terrace turned to the new sound. The words came from the Altiplano Prince. They were his first words of the day.

He straightened to his full, if diminutive, height and called again, "Administrator!"

"Yes," the Administrator replied, using the same language in which the Altiplano Prince addressed him. "What can I do for you, young Prince?"

The others looked at each other quizzically. No one else knew a word of the Altiplano language.

"Administrator, if I understood you properly, you stated the foreigners will take the entire treasure of the kingdom. Is that correct?" asked the Altiplano Prince.

"Yes, that is correct," replied the Administrator, walking over to the engaged couple, a day away from their arranged wedding. "They will take all the treasures of the kingdom—including the virgins." The Administrator shifted his eyes to the elder Princess and then back to the Altiplano Prince.

The Altiplano Prince looked back at the Administrator. He ignored the reference to his fiancée and explained, "Administrator, my marriage contract calls for a dowry upon engagement, regardless of the consummation of the ceremony or the marriage. Regarding the foreigners taste for virgins, the contract includes a specific clause for discovery of non-purity."

"And…" the Administrator replied, arching his eyebrows.

"Therefore," the Altiplano Prince continued, "as a disinterested party, whose people are not yet engaged in an alliance with the enemies of the foreigners and the Incas, who you so nobly and capably represent, I hereby declare my neutrality in this matter and demand fulfillment of my contract." The Altiplano Prince stood up and separated himself from the elder Princess, who glared at him.

Chapter Six

"I presume you mean fulfillment of your dowry contract while there is still something to fulfill it with? Is that what you are demanding?" asked the Administrator.

"Well, yes, stated in its most bold and basic form, yes, that is what I am demanding," replied the Altiplano Prince, adopting the most dignified and regal presence possible with a bruised and bloodied forehead and tattered clothing.

"Well then, I will take up the matter with the foreign General when he arrives, in exactly the terms you have stated," replied the Administrator.

The Altiplano Prince smiled, pleased at how easy it was to accomplish his goal.

"The Altiplano Prince has declared his independence and neutrality in this conflict," the Administrator announced to the royal terrace in Atacameños Kunzan. "According to the terms of his marriage contract, he demands his dowry on the basis of non-completion of the ceremony, due to the impending end of the Atacameños kingdom, and non-purity, due to the impending rape of the kingdom's virgins by the foreigners."

The elder Princess gasped. The King and Queen arose, their faces a mix of rage and fear.

"Guards," the Administrator directed, switching to Inca Quechuan, "move the Altiplano Prince to the far side of the terrace, away from the royal family."

The Administrator turned to the King and Queen, and in perfect, precise Kunzan told them, "I have promised the Altiplano Prince I would bring his case before the foreign General in exactly the terms he presented it to me." He held their gaze for several moments more, as the full meaning of his statement began to arise in their eyes.

*****

The Prince peered over the edge of the roof of the uppermost killing room. He watched the Inca commander at the base of the hill skillfully deploying the rapidly arriving main force. The commander was effective, quickly perceiving the tactical situation and addressing it with forceful, decisive application of his assets.

"The Inca elites and ruling class may have rotted from decadence, but the Inca warriors never did," the Prince thought.

The Inca warriors now arriving were disciplined, reacting instantly to command. Their actions were efficient and direct. They were well trained and carried themselves as only battle-hardened veterans can.

Chapter Six

"What battles hardened these warriors?" the Prince asked his second.

"I know of no Inca battles since the collapse of the empire seven years ago," replied his second.

"These men have fought long and hard since the collapse," the Prince replied, watching the warriors deploy. "They have not been seven years without a battle. No amount of training can make a warrior a warrior. A warrior is formed by battle. And these are warriors."

His second looked at the Prince, mystified.

An arrow split the air between them, not more than a hand away from the Prince's eyes.

They both ducked down, plastered against the rooftop.

"What battles created these warriors?" the Prince asked again as they waited out the barrage.

*****

The General of the North poked his head up just long enough to see the waves of Inca warriors pouring over the first and second barricades and ducked back down.

"How does it look?" asked his second, concern written on his brow.

"It looks like the preliminaries are over, and the main event is about to begin," replied the General. "Gather the commanders, and bring them to me, now!"

The second snapped to attention and replied smartly, "Yes, my General!"

"It is only a matter of time now," thought the General of the North. "I need to get my assets out of here. The North is about to fall."

*****

The little Prince peered around the corner of the meat block. The carving knives were a finger from his nose. The entire area smelled of a mix of freshness and cleanliness, the legacy of his mother's tribe. He heard the voices of the search party rising and falling as they rooted through the food stores; celebrating discoveries, and spitting out disgust at unfamiliar foods.

He waited for them to move on. He just needed a few moments, but he could not risk them spotting him in the passage.

"This is another test of strength," he thought, "The strength of a warrior is in patience."

Chapter Six

He fought the urge to make the dash, and instead waited for the right moment. There was another shriek of delight from the search party as they found more figs, then a grunt and a crash as they threw aside a jar of salted turtle eggs, one of the little Prince's favorites. Finally, the Incas reached the back of the pantry, turned, and moved on.

The little Prince scampered around the corner and through the passage to the liquid stores.

"Only a short distance now," he celebrated. "I will be at the North in but a few moments."

*****

The younger Princess leapt across the last of the temporary, sun-blocking covers over the labyrinth and ran in a low crouch to the far side of the building. She knew this building well; it formed the southern border of her private garden. It was another escape route of her youth, so she knew the handholds and foot steps as well as she knew her own name.

She was down the wall in seconds, thanking the Gods, and amazed she hadn't been spotted in her furtive trek across the roofs of the fortress. She paused at the base, listening for any presence. She knew every sound of this garden. It was her favorite place, her own personal world. She slowly rose and took a long look around at the flowers, ferns, and cactus.

"Now that the sun has begun its southern walk, the friendship cactus will be blooming soon," she mourned, knowing that no Spring would ever be the same after today.

She stooped to pluck a brown, dead leaf from a flower. She admired the bloom for a short moment. She looked down at the dead leaf in her hand and thought of the King and the Queen.

"No, this shall not be!" she proclaimed.

She threw down the leaf and ran to the north wall of the garden. She placed her foot in the familiar place on the bench, grabbed the handhold, and felt her dagger sheath dig into her lower spine.

"One more wall," she thought. "One more climb. One more escape. One more moment, and I will be at the North."

*****

The Prince shook off his second's grasp and poked his head over the roof. The Inca commander had gathered several squads of archers and was positioning them at the base of the killing room feed passageway. He was pointing up the route and giving the archers orders.

Chapter Six

The Prince watched as the pivot wall for killing room two swung aside, and the runner for room three waved and shouted. But, instead of a mob of slaves rushing forth in his direction, he was met with a volley of arrows.

The Prince dropped back down, his face ashen.

"What is it, my Prince?" asked the second gravely. "What did you see?"

"The Inca commander discovered the deception. He is targeting the runners," the Prince lamented, the inevitability of the battle's outcome resonating in his voice.

*****

The heart of the younger Princess nearly burst from her breast. She saw him, her brother! There, on the top of the highest building along the North.

She turned left, changing course from the barricades to the building her brother was on. As she made her way across the low roofs of the outer portions of the royal quarters, she searched for a way to get to him. On the south side of the building where she saw the Prince, there was a clear path, a climbable path, directly up to him. There were plenty of handholds. She knew that she, the best climber in the family, would have no trouble with it.

She climbed down from the low roofs, dropped to the ground, and ran towards her brother. She stopped at the wall blocking the exit of the main passage up the fortress. It stood between her and the building with the Prince. She easily scaled the back of it and peeked over the edge.

Seeing no one, she climbed over the wall and dropped down the other side into the corner. It was a tiny offset alcove just big enough for her small frame, at the top southwest corner of the main passage, opposite the uppermost building she planned to surmount. She pulled back into the shadows to prepare for her climb.

As she caught her breath and examined the building for the best climbing route, she froze. Coming out of the passageway between the uppermost building and the one below was an Inca slave, and he was wearing a red tunic, almost identical to hers.

*****

The Inca commander smiled. Two of the slaves wearing red tunics were dead in the main passage and the movable walls remained open. No more of his men would be wasted by this subterfuge, whatever it was.

Chapter Six

"But what was it?" he thought. "It is worthy of discovery, this trap that ate so many slaves and a few of my raw recruits."

"Two squads, rally!" he commanded. He was instantly surrounded by two squads of his most elite troops.

"Squad one, lead low," he commanded, "Archers one and two follow; squad two, follow high; archers three, cover!"

The men deployed and began a quick march up the main passage.

As they neared the end of the passage, the last pivot wall swung away, revealing a slave wearing a red tunic waving them on.

*****

"Shut down the rooms! Pull the Pumas! Assemble here! Now! Move!" the Prince shouted to his second.

The second did not pause to respond, but instead flew across the roofs toward killing room one, desperate to save the lower squads.
"It is only a matter of time now," the Prince thought. "The North is falling. No one left here will survive."

*****

The younger Princess held her breath, afraid to move, certain the slave would see her. The slave turned and faced downhill. The younger Princess peeked around the corner to see down the main passageway and saw an advancing mass of Inca warriors, arrows strung and blades at the ready.

The slave in the red tunic greeted the Incas with shouts and waves, urging them on, into the uppermost building.

"They will kill my brother!" the Princess thought. "He has no idea the Incas are coming. He will have no chance!"

The young Princess reached back and pulled her dagger. It was not the best throwing knife, it was inherently unbalanced by the decorative stones, but it would have to do. She brought it round and prepared to stride into her throw, targeting the slave's heart, just as she practiced so many times.

Suddenly, the slave stopped shouting and staggered back. The red tunic over his chest sprouted a forest of arrows. He stumbled back, then over, back again, then over, falling less than a stride away from the Princess.

He looked up, the light fading from his eyes, then, in a burst, they ignited again.

Chapter Six

"My Princess!" he gurgled, blood sprouting from his mouth.

*****

The Prince poked up his head and looked down. He feared the worst and saw it confirmed. The runner was perforated, lying twisted into the far, upper corner of the passage. The killing rooms were done. The main force of the Inca warriors was yet to even be engaged. The battle was over.

The Prince began to slide back down when a movement caught his eye. There, in the dark corner of the passageway, was another slave in a red tunic, another runner.

"Who could that be?" the Prince thought. "All the runners have been killed."

Then the runner bent forward, and his heart stopped. It was not a runner. It was his sister. It was the younger Princess.

*****

The runner's words bubbled with blood. The younger Princess struggled to understand.

"Lead them? Is that what you are saying?" the Princess asked, bending closer.

The runner nodded weakly, struggling to give her the message.

"Lead them where? Into the building?" the Princess asked.

The runner nodded again, weaker still, his strength fading.

He gurgled out another phrase. She couldn't understand it. She thought she heard "push" but wasn't sure.

"Again, please, I could not understand you. Push what? What should I push?" the Princess pressed, seeing the runner would not last much longer.

"Flower, push…" the light in the runner's eyes went out. It was his end. The younger Princess looked up. The Inca warriors were no more than thirty strides away. They had sheathed their blades, and only a few bows were ready. They were not in kill mode, now they were in search mode. They were looking for something.

The little Princess knew what they would find. They would find her brother.

Chapter Six

*****

"Two! Go Back! Two! Climb out! Don't come here!" the Prince screamed over the roof's edge.

She could not hear him; his voice was drowned out by the battle of the barricades raging next to her.

The Prince rose up and shouted, "Two! Go Back! Climb out!"

An arrow grazed his shoulder, drawing blood. Another zinged by his ear. The Inca archers had spotted him. They were reloading from their quivers and drawing on him.

The Prince dropped to the roof, tears welling in his eyes.

"I have killed my sister!" he wailed.

*****

The younger Princess looked up with the flight of the arrows and saw her brother dropping down below the edge of the roof.

The Incas were distracted from her. She knew what she had to do.

She ran across to the passage leading into the building and began to shout at the Incas. The archers drew down on her and let loose a volley. Before the arrows arrived, she turned and ran.

*****

The Prince's second slammed down the roof trap door of killing room two and headed for the third. The Pumas from the first killing room were already on the roof and headed after him, the squad from the second would be up in seconds. They all knew the reality. No one left here would survive.

"Only a few more short moments," the second thought, "and I will have all four rooms stopped and the squads safe."

*****

"General of the North, I have a field action report!" the voice from below shouted.

The General dropped his head just below the edge of the wall, as Inca arrows sliced the air above him. The voice was familiar, but impossible. He looked down and almost fell off the observation ledge.

Chapter Six

"Little Prince! By the Gods! What are you doing here?" the General shouted while jumping down. "And, look at you! You look as if you've been dipped in mud! What an appearance for a junior warrior!"

"My General, it was part of the disguise," he began, then stopped, composed himself and started again.

"I was given a secret mission by the King. I formed a squad of five junior warriors. By using the route of the falcon, we retrieved the arrows from the battle of the South. With those arrows, we rearmed the East," the little Prince reported in crisp military form, maintaining discipline despite the message screaming inside his head to escape.

"Casualties?" inquired the General formally.

"One foreign warrior," the little Prince replied stoically. He felt his head was ready to explode. He must tell the General!

"Junior warrior, you and your squad did well. The battle would have been lost at the East if not for those arrows. You saved the kingdom!" the General proclaimed. "But, that mission is over. You should be in safety back in the royal quarters. You should be there, not here in the battle. You are in danger. I must order you to retreat and help the King to analyze the battle from above. After the battle, I will meet you there, and you can tell me all the details, especially about the casualty!"

"My General," the little Prince replied quickly. "I will comply with your orders, but first I must file an additional scouting report."

"Very well," replied the General, ducking down and grabbing the Prince to protect him from a hurtled stone. "But, make it quick, you are in danger here."

"My General," exclaimed the little Prince, standing tall and looking up into his eyes, "The Incas are in the royal household. The foreigners are also there. They came by the way of the condor, by the methods my brother thwarted in the last battle."

The General of the North stopped breathing. He only had one thought, "Two!"

*****

The Administrator turned away from the Inca warrior disguised as an Atacameños who was flagging signals to the Inca commander below. The Administrator marched to the King and Queen. He stood before them and addressed them directly.

"King and Queen," the Administrator began, "time now draws short. My men have searched the entire royal quarters three times with three different teams. My commanders below report no success in their

Chapter Six

searches there." He paused and looked at each of them gravely, then continued. "Every one of my men has strict orders to find and hold your children. The children have not been found. I need to know where they are, and I need to know now!" The veins on his neck were bulging. It was the first time he had shown emotion.

"And what, pray tell, would make you think that if I knew I would ever tell you?" asked the Queen.

"Dear Queen," replied the Administrator, "if you live to see tomorrow, those may be the words you most regret saying in your entire life."

*****

The younger Princess ran into the room and stopped short. Ahead of her lay a broad avenue climbing up to the royal quarters, topped by a grand staircase leading directly to the royal terrace. It was stunning, it was beautiful, it was mesmerizing, and, she knew, it was not real. There was no such avenue in Pukara de Quitor.

She heard the Inca warriors behind her running up the passageway, mere strides away, their blades clanking against the stone walls.

"What did he mean?" she thought quickly, her mind racing. "Press the flower, press the flower. What flower, where?"

The young Princess scanned the scene. There were flowers scattered about, from one end to the other: water flowers, high pasture flowers, flowers on shrubs, flowers on trees, flowers in pots, flowers of all types, in all places, but, she realized in a flash, only one cactus and only one cactus flower.

She ran forward and pushed hard on the cactus flower just as the first Inca reached the doorway behind her. Her hand slid in, the wall gave way, and she tumbled in, the center-pivoting wall swinging around and clicking into place. She heard the room fill with shouting men. She heard thuds as they banged off the wall on either side of her and felt the center-pivoting wall shift as they ran headlong into it.

Suddenly, the light leaking in through the cracks on either side of the center-pivoting wall went black. There was a sliding sound and a loud clunk, then a strange, long whoosh followed by a hollow boom, and the entire building shook. As the echoes of that massive sound faded from her ears, she heard faint screams to her left that rapidly melted away and were overwhelmed by the noise of the battle to her right.

Her tiny chamber was black except for some light seeping through from above. She heard shouts from up there, and running feet, then everything was silent; everything except the pounding of her heart.

*****

Chapter Six

"The commanders are ready," the General of the North's second reported.

The General swung around, his head still pounding with the news.

"Come, this way," the second motioned, "it is out of the line of fire."

The General turned and looked at the little Prince. "Follow," was all he said.

*****

The Prince watched as the last Puma team climbed out, counting them one by one.

"How many?" he asked his second.

"Only the runners," the second replied.

"Only the runners," the Prince thought. "Only the runners. I watched the last runner killed. But then I heard the fourth killing room cycle. Why did the Incas enter the room if there was no runner?"

"Squad leader!" the Prince called to the final Puma climbing out of killing room four. "Was your last cycle full?"

"Yes, my Prince!" the squad leader replied. "And, it was a load of real Inca warriors; there were no slaves."

"Then she is there!" the Prince cried. He dove for the trap door, pushed the squad leader out of the way, and slid down the ladder.

*****

The younger Princess felt the center-pivoting wall in front of her.

"If there was a way in, there must be a way out," she thought.

She worked systematically, from the upper left of the door to the lower right.

She was halfway down when she heard running and shouting above her.

"There!" she thought in triumph. "There is a protruding stone."

She shoved on the stone, and the wall pivoted around again, just as the trap door above her opened.

*****

Chapter Six

"Two!" screamed the Prince, as he watched her disappear, swept by the center-pivoting wall into the killing room.

"By the Gods!" screamed the Prince. "Get out of my way! The room is not reset!"

*****

The center-pivoting wall pushed the younger Princess out into nothing. All before her was black and to her left was open space, a broad view of the cliffs on the far side of the canyon. She fell straight down about half a man, hit the sloping floor of the killing room, and began sliding left, towards the way of the Gods, to the river, far, far below.

*****

The Prince leapt down the ladder, crashing through the bottom three rungs. He turned and pounded on the center-pivoting wall, shouting, "Two! Two! Two!"

He heard her scream fading, off to his left, towards the river.

He looked up at the Puma team crowding around the trap door and demanded, "Where is the release? It is not in the same position as room one! Where is the release?"

*****

The General of the North faced his senior leaders.

"Commanders! Listen carefully!" he ordered. "This briefing will only be delivered once."

He waited for their attention, then proceeded. "Our tactical situation is deteriorating. We have an unconfirmed report of a major strategic threat.

He paused to ensure they all understood the implications of his words. Then, he ordered, "Deploy your forces for a fighting retreat, maximum delay, maximum counter fire. Use all pre-staged arms and all pre-planned maneuvers. Go. Now."

As they turned to leave, the General reached out to his senior commander and pulled him aside. The General directed, "Commander, have your flag man signal the royal terrace that we need a hot meal immediately. I want to know the reply."

"My General, I don't think I heard you correctly," the commander replied, leaning in closer. "What was the message to send to the royal terrace?"

Chapter Six

The General repeated, "Flag a message to the royal terrace that we need a hot meal immediately. I need to know the reply. Do it! Now!"

The commander stood to attention and snapped, "Yes, my General! Immediately!"

*****

The younger Princess slid down the slick floor, accelerating towards the edge. She began to smell the fresh air of the valley. She was leaving the stench of battle behind.

"No!" she screamed. "No!"

The Princess reached behind her, pulled her dagger, and, with all her strength, stabbed it into the killing room floor. Her momentum nearly wrenched her shoulder out of its socket, but her grip held—barely.

She snuck a look down. Her feet were hanging over the edge in open space. She saw the river glistening in the sun. It was a very long way down to the river.

Her fingers began to slip.

*****

"I will tell you!" the squad leader yelled down. "But be careful, the wall will pivot you out just like her. There is an emergency grab strap on the left side of the door. Hold on to it, and we will reset the floor."

"Where?" repeated the Prince. "Where is the release?"

"Lower right quadrant, a little below waist high," yelled the squad leader.

The Prince reached down and felt in the lower right quadrant of the door until he found the trigger. He pushed it and reached left for the strap as he was shoved out into space.

*****

The younger Princess looked up at her right hand. The gap between her fingers and her palm was growing wider.

She reached up with her left hand, but was unable to get high enough to touch the dagger. Her left shoulder was hanging down lower than her right, and her reach would never be enough.

"I've got to pivot my shoulders," she thought.

Chapter Six

She mustered all of her strength, took a deep breath, and then lost it in a gasp, as above her the center-pivoting wall rotated and spit out her brother, who fell towards her.

*****

The Prince looked down at his feet and saw her. She was hanging onto something, something stuck into the floor. The brightness of the canyon behind her made it difficult to see after the dark of the runner chamber. She was just a silhouette, hanging in brightly-lit space.

"Hold on!" yelled the Prince, as he worked to improve his grip on the strap. "Hold on, Two! The Pumas are resetting the room!"

"I am trying, but my hand is slipping!" the young Princess yelled back. "I don't know how much longer I can hold. I cannot pivot my shoulders to get my left hand on the dagger!"

"So, that is how she did it!" thought the Prince. "We put hundreds of slaves and at least a few score Inca warriors through these rooms today, and she is the first to stop her fall with a simple dagger. My little sister once again proves she is smarter, faster, and better than all the rest, especially the boys!"

"Hold on!" repeated the Prince. "It will only be a moment before the floor resets!"

The younger Princess looked up at her brother, hanging above her. She saw his face clearly, his eyes like bright, shining jewels.

Her fingers slipped again, and her focus shifted back to her hand on the dagger. The jewels in the handle were sharp, polished, and slick. They were not helping matters.

"Brother, my Prince!" the young Princess yelled. "My hand is slipping, but I must tell you this, there are Incas in the royal quarters! I saw them with my own eyes! I came here to tell you!"

"You can tell me when you are in arms!" shouted the Prince. "You hold onto that dagger! You will need it to kill the Inca who touches my King!"

The young Princess smiled through the pain. She loved her brother so. There was only one other she loved more.

She closed her eyes and grimaced. It wouldn't be long now; only a moment or two, and it would be over.

The Prince saw her eyes close. He knew it would be soon.

"Two!" he shouted. "Two! Hold on! There is someone you must hold on for! He needs to see you! He needs to tell you something!"

The young Princess's eyes opened. She looked at her brother. She thought of the General of the North.

Her grip tightened.

The floor began to move up.

*****

"My General!" the commander shouted, running into the briefing area. "The signal officer reports that the royal terrace replies with 'The llama has four heads.' Is it a code? What is the meaning of that?"

"The meaning of that message is a junior warrior is always to be trusted," replied the General.

"I don't understand." replied the commander. "What shall we do? What are your orders?"

"You have my orders, commander," replied the General. "Now go and execute them."

The General turned to the little Prince and explained, "I did not doubt you, little Prince, but a General must always confirm his scouting reports."

"I understand, General," replied the little Prince. "When I am a General, I will do the same."

The General smiled softly and began to turn away.

"General," the little Prince interrupted. "Forgive me. Please, indulge me one question before you return to the battle."

"Yes, my Prince," the General replied, the soft smile returning. "What is your question?"

"How long will you continue to do what the enemy expects you to do, thereby concealing your knowledge of the strategic situation?" asked the little Prince, as if in a war game in a council of generals.

"Until I can talk with the only man in the entire kingdom other than you who could grasp what I am doing!" the General replied, his smile broadening across his face.

*****

Chapter Six

There was a rustle in the background. The Administrator turned and took it in. He looked back and announced, "The pleasantries have ended and I fear the day will sadly deteriorate from this point forward."

The Administrator glanced back to the noise and then implored, "King, say goodbye to your Queen. This will be your last opportunity. In only a moment you will be leaving her side for the last time."

The Administrator gave them a thin smile and walked towards the new arrivals.

The Next Name

Seven

"My God!" exclaimed the foreign General. "Couldn't you find us a place out of the sun? Do you mean to tell me they sit out here? That this is their idea of a royal terrace?"

"Yes, they are degenerate in every way, General," replied the Administrator in Spanish, bowing deeply.

"Please, follow me," he continued. "We have prepared a place for you out of the sun." He led the General over to the thrones, still occupied by the King and Queen.

"Out, out you pigs!" the Administrator shouted in Spanish, gesturing towards the King and Queen. In Kunzan he added, under his breath, "King and Queen, please move quickly, lest his anger begin so early as to make the rest of the day even uglier than it is likely to be."

He turned to the General and added in Spanish, "They are such slow creatures. Quite docile really, like swine, but slow to react, as you saw in our battle today."

He turned to the King and Queen, still frozen in their seats, and urged in Kunzan, "If you don't move immediately, he will kill you where you sit. I have seen it before. Please, for the sake of your children, move, now!"

The King and Queen rose, stepped down from the thrones, walked to the eldest Princess, and took the seats of the Prince and younger Princess.

"And you expect me to sit here, where those animals have soiled?" asked the General incredulously.

"No, no, no," soothed the Administrator. He turned to the nearest Inca warrior and yelled in Quechuan, "Rip down that tapestry and bring it here!"

The Inca warrior turned and used his dagger to slice off the anchor points of the 400-year old tapestry. He gathered it up, brought it to the throne, and, following the Administrators gestures, draped it over the King's throne.

Chapter Seven

The General ascended the throne, glanced down on the battle raging below, turned to the Administrator, and commanded, "Get the treasure out here and let's get this over with. I want to be out of this Hell-hole before dinner."

*****

The younger Princess was almost unconscious from exhaustion. As the floor rose, she became less and less connected with the world around her and slipped further and further away.

"My Princess!" shouted the Puma from the trap door above. "Your feet! Your feet! Pull up your feet!"

The Princess heard voices, far away, saying something, something urgent. She could not understand what they were saying; she just wanted to let go, let go of the pain.

The Prince looked down as the gap closed between the raising floor and the base of the outer wall. His sister's feet dangled over the edge of the floor, now less than half a man below the wall and rising. He waited another count, released the strap and slid down the floor on his back, his feet raised. As he slid closer, he saw his feet were too low, they were below the wall.

He glanced out and saw the cliffs on the far side of the canyon, the brightness nearly blinding him.

The wall was approaching quickly, but the floor was rising too slowly. He had misjudged. He released too early. The Prince accelerated towards the gap, the yawning chasm below sucking him in like a sinkhole in the great salt of the south.

*****

The General of the North raised his head and looked out from his command post. He saw all the Puma squads hunkered down on the top of killing room four, ready to deploy down the escape ladder.

He turned to his second and ordered, "You are in command. Follow the plan. Conserve your resources. I shall return."

He turned to the little Prince, motioned him forward, and said, "It is time. Come."

*****

"This?" the General shouted in dismay. "I risked my life climbing up here for this?" He looked up at the Administrator and glowered.

"Oh, I assure you General, there is more," the Administrator cooed in Spanish. "The Atacameños have been collecting treasure for hundreds, for thousands of years! There is much more! Here, examine this chest of gold while you wait. My men are emptying the treasury for your pleasure. I will interview the King to ensure they are hiding nothing."

He bowed lowly once again and moved over to the King, Queen and elder Princess.

He turned to them to speak but before he could begin the assault began.

"You groveling scum!" screamed the elder Princess. "First you ruin my feast, next you ruin my wedding, and now you give away my dowry to this filthy pig foreigner!"

The Administrator was taken aback, but recovered quickly. "Ah, your dowry, thank you for reminding me of that matter, my dear Princess," he replied with a wry smile.

Then he turned to the Queen and confided, "I knew she would be a challenge, but now I fear the very worst for her."

*****

The Prince rolled onto his right side and raised his left leg as high as he could. His left foot barely caught the lower edge of the wall, stopping him abruptly, his knee absorbing the shock. He looked over at the Princess, her eyes glazed and unfocused. She smiled weakly and released the dagger.

The greased floor was so slick that even with only the slight remaining angle, she began to slide over the edge.

"No!" screamed the Prince.

He reached out and grabbed her limp right wrist with his left hand. Her wrist was slick with her blood. The jewels of the dagger handle had pierced her palm and blood was everywhere. Her wrist slipped in his grasp. She slid further down the ramp. Her legs dangled over the end of the ramp, which continued its inexorable climb. He grabbed her wet hand and felt her blood oozing into his grip, lubricating it.

The Prince looked down, unsure what to do. If he held on, in a short moment, she would be sliced in half. If he let go, she would fall to her death with the Incas below.

*****

The Administrator motioned to the far side of the royal terrace.

Chapter Seven

"Come," he called in Altiplano, "come and make your case before the General."

The Altiplano Prince rose, straightened his torn clothing as best he could, attempted to wipe away the crusted blood from his forehead, and strode over to appear before the throne.

"General," the Administrator began in Spanish, "you have a petitioner."

Without lifting his head from examining the chest of gold on his lap, the General glanced up at the Administrator and the Altiplano Prince.

"And what petition does a bedraggled creature such as this bring to a conqueror?" asked the General distractedly, beginning to count another stack of gold, the pieces clicking steadily.

"Prince of the Altiplano, would you like to restate your case or do you think I can do so accurately?" the Administrator formally inquired of the Altiplano Prince in his native language.

"I can observe by your professionalism that you are quite capable of accurately presenting my case, dear Administrator," the Altiplano Prince replied, in his most dignified and courtly manner. "Please proceed."

"The Altiplano Prince states the following," the Administrator began in Spanish, in a purely bureaucratic tone. "His marriage contract states that he is owed a dowry by the Atacameños court regardless of consummation of the ceremony or the marriage. He perceives that there is a very small likelihood of the ceremony proceeding as planned tomorrow and thus seeks his dowry from the Atacameños treasury forthwith."

"A marriage, eh?" replied the General, his eyes rising to meet the Administrator's, the clicking of his counting paused.

"Yes, General, to the eldest daughter of the King," the Administrator replied, regret evident in his voice despite his best efforts to conceal it.

"Hmmm," the General intoned, warming to the topic. "A marriage means a bride, and a bride means a virgin. That is a topic that is close to my heart." He looked up from his chest and turned his head to the eldest Princess, who shot daggers with her eyes in return.

"And a most spirited virgin, at that!" the General chuckled. "They always make the most fun. There is nothing like spirit. It keeps them going for the first little while." He looked back down and continued his counting, the pieces resuming their steady clicking.

Chapter Seven

The Altiplano Prince cleared his throat. The clicking continued.

The Administrator glanced at the Altiplano Prince, held out his hands, and raised his shoulders, a look of helpless resignation on his face.

The Altiplano Prince cleared his throat again. The clicking continued.

The Altiplano Prince could take the rudeness of the General no longer. He urged in Altiplano, "Dear sir, I am of a royal house and demand the respect due to me. I ask you to address my petition so that I may take leave of this court and return to my home with both my dowry and honor intact."

The General ignored him. The clicking continued.

The Altiplano Prince fumed. His face grew red. His hands clenched and unclenched. He turned to the Administrator and shouted in Altiplano, "I demand you translate my statement to the foreigner. Translate every word."

The Administrator looked at the Altiplano Prince, paused, shrugged and turned back to the General.

"General," he began in Spanish. The General did not look up or pause his counting.

"The Altiplano Prince states he is of a royal house and demands the respect due to him. He asks you to address his petition so that he may take leave of this court and return to his home with both his dowry and honor intact," the Administrator translated faithfully.

The clicking continued, the pace never wavering.

The Altiplano Prince could stand it no longer. He stamped his foot in frustration.

The General's counting paused. He looked up at the Altiplano Prince and than at the Administrator.

The General set the chest of gold aside and stood up. He towered above the Altiplano Prince, who shriveled before him.

"So," the General thundered, "you want the respect you deserve, you wish to depart, and you want your dowry in a safe place, is that correct?"

The Administrator translated, and the Altiplano Prince nodded nervously.

The General stepped down from the throne to the terrace, directly in front of the Altiplano Prince, who was now visibly shaking.

Chapter Seven

The General reached back and scooped out a handful of gold from the chest he was counting. He held up the gold in front of the Altiplano Prince's face, pieces tumbling from his hand to the terrace's inlaid tile below.

"Is this an adequate dowry, Prince?" the General bellowed, glaring down at the cowering Altiplano Prince. The Administrator translated.

The Prince nodded his head again and bleated, "Yes, General, it is most adequate. I will be happy to take that dowry and be on my way. I am, we are, my people are, neutral in this entire matter. I wish, we wish, nothing but peaceful relations with you."

The Administrator translated every word while the Altiplano Prince shook below the General, sweat dripping from his bruised and bloodied face.

"Good, I am glad to learn that your intentions are peaceful and that this dowry is adequate," snarled the General, while withdrawing his dagger. "I shall place it where it will be safe."

In two quick moves, the General slit open the belly of the Altiplano Prince and shoved the handful of gold inside.

He stood over the bloody, spasm-wracked body and exulted, holding his hands high. He turned to those on the royal terrace and smiled, blood running down his arm.

He turned back to the dying Prince and shouted, "And, now you can depart!" He kicked the body off the front of the terrace.

The foreign General ascended the throne, wiped the blood from his hands on the tapestry, put the chest of gold back on his lap, resumed his counting, and, without looking up, growled to the Administrator, "I am ready for the next petitioner."

*****

The General of the North peered up at the top of killing room four. All the Pumas had turned away, and none were keeping watch down the back side.

"This is very unlike the Pumas," the little Prince commented. "They are the best trained and most disciplined of all warriors."

"Yes," the General agreed, "it is most unlike the Pumas. There must be something very important happening for them to drop their guard like this."

Chapter Seven

"Squad leader!" the General called. The leader of his personal guard responded immediately.

"Get a man up there and find out what is happening. I need to see the Prince. Tell him it is of the utmost importance. The kingdom depends on his presence."

The squad leader turned and motioned to his fastest climber. They conferred, and the warrior ascended the ladder in a blur and disappeared over the top.

In less than a moment, his face appeared over the edge. His expression was grim. He yelled down but the message was lost in the din of battle. Seeing no response, he mounted the ladder and slid down most of the way, destroying his hands in the process. He ran in a crouch to the command position and reported, blood dripping from his hands.

"My General!" he reported. "It is the Prince and the young Princess. They are trapped in the killing room. The young Princess is sliding over the edge!"

*****

"Two!" the Prince screamed. There was no response. He leaned toward her and screamed again "Two!" There was a faint flicker in her eyes.

"Two, I need you! We need you!" Her eyes focused on him. He knew she could not resist a call of assistance.

"Two! I need you!" he yelled again.

Her eyes hardened and came alive.

"What can I do to help you?" she asked, strength returning to her voice.

"I can't hold you much longer! I need your help!" the Prince pleaded.

"What can I do? How can I help you?" Two replied, echoing his urgency. He knew he had her now.

"Look at my legs. Can you see how they are positioned?" the Prince asked. "I need you to mirror me. I need you to roll to your left side and wedge your right leg against the wall, just as my left is. Pull it up to your waist and wedge it against the wall. Do it quickly! Do it now!"

Her blood pumped into his grip; it seeped out and dripped down onto the slick killing room floor, formed pools on the polished surface, and ran in rivulets out over the edge to the canyon floor below. He knew it would end very soon—very, very soon.

Chapter Seven

"Yes, brother, I see, I am ready—now!" the younger Princess replied. She rolled to her left side as her right hand slipped from his. She drew up her leg as she slid towards the open edge. She jammed her right foot into the base of the wall, dislodging dust and small pebbles that bounced off the end of the floor and launched out into canyon. She stopped sliding.

The floor continued its climb.

"Sister, your leg!" he Prince shouted. "Pull up your left leg!"

The younger Princess jerked up her left leg just as the killing room floor banged home, locking into place for the last time.

They lay there panting, looking into each other's eyes, speechless.

After several long moments, the Prince reached up and rocked the dagger back and forth to release it from the floor. He wiped the blood from the grip on his tunic.

"Here," he grinned, handing her the dagger, "the King would be disappointed if we rescued him without this."

*****

The General of the North pushed the Pumas aside from the trap door and stared down into the dark killing room below. His eyes could not adjust; all he could see was dimness.

"Two!" he shouted, "Two! Are you there? Are you all right? Two!"

The Prince smiled at his sister and announced, "There is someone here to see you. Is the younger Princess receiving guests this afternoon?"

His sister reached out and punched him softly in the shoulder, then yelped with pain from her ripped palm.

"Yes, General, she is fine!" the Prince yelled in reply. "We are coming now! Ready the Pumas for cover and fighting retreat! We have a mission!"

*****

The King caught the eye of the Administrator and motioned for him.

"General," the Administrator oozed solicitously, "by your leave, I shall seek further treasures from the King." He bowed lowly and moved over to the King.

"Administrator," the King queried, "what is my fate?"

"Your life is forfeit, dear King," replied the Administrator. "It has been so since the day you defeated him earlier this year. He swore revenge on you and your kingdom."

"What is the fate of my kingdom?" asked the King, unmoved by his death sentence.

"The details are still in play," replied the Administrator, "But, if the foreign General keeps his word, it will largely come to me."

The Administrator smiled at the King and glanced at the Queen, who glared at him, hissing in response, "You defile the kingdom with every step you take, you maggot!"

"Dear Queen," soothed the Administrator, "please do not let present circumstances harden your views."

"Administrator," interrupted the King, "what is the fate of my family?"

"That," replied the Administrator, his expression grim, "has yet to be determined."

*****

They gathered in the command post.

"Second, situation report," the General of the North ordered matter-of-factly.

"The General of the East is missing and presumed a casualty. The labyrinth is nearly overrun. The last barricade is falling now. As you know, the killing rooms are abandoned. All forces are taking up fighting retreat positions at ring level one. Arrow stocks are at critical levels. There are no available reserves. All assets are committed to the battle," the second reported.

"Thank you. Your orders are to continue with the plan. Issue blades to the archers who have depleted their quivers. Carry on," the General ordered, and then turned to the group.

The Prince spoke first.

"General," he began. "I believe an assault by the Pumas and five of your best squads can rescue the King and Queen. I have worked out a plan."

The General held up a hand to his best friend, cutting him off. The General turned to the little Prince, who was applying raw aloe to his burned palms.

"Little Prince, what are the standing orders of a warrior leader?" he asked.

Chapter Seven

The little Prince snapped to attention and replied with precision, "The first standing order of a warrior leader is to know the enemy.

"The second standing order of a warrior leader is to equip, train, and prepare his forces to effectively oppose the enemy and defend the kingdom.

"The third standing order of a warrior leader is to maintain vigilance of defense.

"The fourth standing order of a warrior leader is to actively seek knowledge of the unknown aspects of the battle space.

"The fifth standing order of a warrior leader is to be overwhelming in attack.

"The sixth standing order of a warrior leader is to encourage flexibility and innovation in his fighting force.

"The seventh standing order of a warrior leader is to retain an effective fighting force to ensure the continuance of the names."

The General then asked, "Little Prince, given our tactical and strategic situation, what do you believe is the course of action that reflects the standing orders of a warrior leader?"

The little Prince paused. He looked up at his brother, his hero, and then back to the General.

"We must retain an effective fighting force to ensure the continuance of the names," the little Prince replied.

"I concur," the General replied.

The General looked to the Prince and declared, "My Prince, I have sworn my oath to uphold the standing orders of a warrior leader. I must deploy my assets accordingly."

The Prince looked at the General, and a slow smile spread across his face. "He finally believes it," he thought.

"General, you choose wisely," replied the Prince. "I will formulate a plan based on my available assets." The Prince glanced at his sister. The General followed his gaze, and then looked back at the Prince. They shared a small smile.

"I think of the two fighting forces, you shall have the most formidable assets," the General lauded.

*****

Chapter Seven

The Inca warriors grunted as they put the large chest at the feet of the foreign General. The General paused his counting, glanced at it, and looked up at his commander escorting the treasure.

"How much more?" he asked.

"Not enough to make dealing with these stinking pigs worthwhile," replied the commander.

"Did they steal from us?" demanded the General.

"The treasury seal was in place when I arrived," the commander replied. "As agreed, the Incas waited for us before entering. The treasury was full to overflowing when opened. There was no evidence of tampering or theft. I escorted every delivery, and my guards remain in place at the treasury. What you have before you and what remains below is the extent of the kingdom's treasures."

"They expect me to buy a duchy with this?" the General complained, disgust dripping from his voice.

He turned to the commander in dismay and lamented, "How will I ever wed a Princess with such a pauper's wealth?"

The commander grimaced, sharing the General's dismay. His portion was smaller than the General's and he shared the same ambitions.

"Administrator!" the General shouted.

The Administrator scurried to the foot of the throne.

"Yes, General," he groveled.

"We traveled over endless deserts. We scaled mountains. We hungered. We thirsted. We suffered the indignity of association with you and your kind. And this is our reward? This pittance?" the General spat out the last words, spittle splattering the Administrator's face.

"The Atacameños are the richest kingdom of the known south, General. They have ruled here for centuries, for millennia; there are none wealthier south of Cusco," the Administrator replied earnestly, secure in the defense of his facts.

"What do these pigs know of wealth?" the General screamed, rising on the throne.

"What do they know of kingdoms? Where are their palaces? Where are their ballrooms? Where are their jewel encrusted carriages? These pigs know nothing of kingdoms! They know nothing of palaces! They know nothing of life! They know nothing of nothing!" he screamed. He threw a handful of gold down on the tile of the royal terrace, scattering it across the floor, and slumped back down into the throne.

"I shall seek additional treasures from the King," the Administrator promised. He bowed and moved back over to the King.

"What was he screaming in his strange tongue?" asked the King, worried the General was about to commit more violence on his court.

"It was the same speech he gives everywhere. He says that humans only became intelligent a couple of centuries ago, and that the only smart humans in the world are in Europe. They all think that way. They consider themselves a higher form of life, a more evolved human. They believe they are superior in every way to every other person in the world. They believe that is their place, above all others, and always will be," replied the Administrator, his mouth forming a crooked smile. Then he added, "If they weren't so dangerous to themselves and to others, it would be quite humorous."

"Why did he throw the gold across the terrace?" asked the King.

"He is disappointed in the treasure. He seeks to duplicate the riches of his peers who enslaved my people. He desires another mountain of wealth that he can force slaves to extract. Nothing short of that will please him," the Administrator answered, keeping a wary eye on the General.

"Why doesn't he just take the treasure and go?" asked the Queen, finally joining in her husband's tactic of engaging the Administrator.

"He waits for one additional treasure," replied the Administrator hollowly.

"What treasure is that?" asked the King. "The vaults are nearly empty. What remains is no more valuable than what lies before him."

"Oh, the treasure he awaits is not gold," replied the Administrator, turning to the King. "It is the Prince."

*****

Eight

The Prince watched as the General of the North approached his younger sister. He saw her eyes illuminate with love and the General's return it in full.

The Prince remembered the first time he saw that look on the cliffs above the valley. It was the three of them, on another adventure, this time climbing to the top of the cliffs to watch the moon set. They could have watched from the royal terrace or anywhere they pleased, but, seeking something new, seeking a challenge, they decided it could only be done from the east facing cliffs above the mountains of salt.

And, of course, they determined they could not just walk up the trade route to the top, they must climb to the top, like true adventurers. And, as usual, his little sister led the way. She was by far the best climber among them, and she beat them to the top by a long while.

She sat on the cliff's edge, swinging her feet, laughing at them as they struggled up the vertical face. She dropped small pebbles on them, just to torment them, meeting each of their curses with another giggle. No matter what threat they screamed, from immersion in llama urine to shaving her hair, the pebbles dribbled down, one by one.

When they finally reached the top and pulled themselves over the edge, sweaty and covered in dust, she just laughed, melting their hearts with her smile. It was there, at that spot, as she wiped the cheek of his best friend with her hand, that he first saw the look in her eyes. It was the look of love.

As they sat on the cliff that night, watching the full moon sink into the salt of the south, they talked of life, of their futures, and of the future of the kingdom.

The Prince and his best friend discussed the need to build the young boys of the kingdom. The boys needed a way to learn the old ways. They were getting softened by the life of the city and the oasis. They needed to know the things that the ancients knew, that the King's generation knew. The kingdom needed a way to pass on the teachings. That was the beginning of the junior warriors, in that place, on that night.

As the moon dropped lower, they talked of their friendship and of their families. The Prince's younger sister despaired as to always being second behind her demanding and ostentatious older sister.

The pair saw their chance to revenge the pebble shower of their climb and immediately deemed her eternally second, always "Two." The name stuck, and it was the only way they addressed her outside of formal settings from that night until this very day.

Across the command post, the Prince watched as the General reached out.

"Two," the General of the North spoke softly, touching her arm. "Two, I must apologize for my actions earlier today. I was impetuous and ill-tempered. I beg you to forgive me."

"Oh, dear one," the younger Princess replied. "There is no need to beg, I forgive you. How can I not forgive you? I love you."

The General reached out and took her in his arms, kissed her cheek and whispered in her ear. "And I love you. I always have and I always will, from now until eternity."

The General pulled back and looked in her eyes.

"But now, I must go," he resolved.

"As I must," she replied, her eyes moist.

"Go with my love," she confirmed, touching his cheek in the same way and place as that night on the cliffs above the mountains of salt.

"And, you with mine," he replied, his eyes full.

"Two," gently interjected the Prince, stepping up to them. "Forgive me, but the General must depart if there is any chance for his team."

"Where will you go? How will you go?" the Princess asked the General, her eyes clouding with concern. "There is no way out of the Pukara de Quitor."

"There is only one way out," replied the General, "the route of the Gods."

*****

"I am sorry, my Queen," the King whispered, his voice thick with remorse.

Chapter Eight

"Your legacy is not one worthy of sorrow, my King," replied the Queen, her eyes strong. "You have been a good man, a faithful and loyal partner, a wise father, and an enlightened King. Your name will be revered for centuries."

"The names," the King mourned. "The names. The names shall end with me!"

*****

"Pumas!" the General of the North shouted, struggling to be heard above the battle closing in on them. "I ask for volunteers. This will be a mission of indefinite length. It will separate you from your family and friends. It will be filled with hardship. It will be a long battle against even longer odds. I ask for volunteers to join me in the highlands to continue the battle against those who seek to destroy our kingdom. There is no dishonor in staying. Those who wish to join me, step forward."

The Pumas stepped forward as one. A small smile played on the General's lips.

"I expected as much!" he cheered. "Come, gather for the briefing. Our time is very short and our route most perilous."

*****

"Do you know the plan?" the Prince asked again.

"I repeated it flawlessly five times!" snapped the younger Princess. "What do you think?"

"Good," the Prince replied, casting her a sideways glance. "Now, prepare to abandon it."

They stepped to the end of the dark passageway.

"What do you mean?" she demanded. "I just spent all this time memorizing it, and now you want me to abandon it?"

"Two, no plan survives contact with reality," the Prince whispered in reply. "When we arrive, things will be different than our plan assumes. Things will happen that we did not, and could not, anticipate. We will need to adapt to the reality of the situation. If so, we must modify or abandon the plan and improvise a new one. If we cling stubbornly and rigidly to a plan that does not match reality, we only guarantee failure."

"How will I know when to modify or abandon the plan?" asked the younger Princess, suddenly seized by doubts.

The Prince replied, "When reality does not match your anticipations."

"Well, that started about mid-day!" the younger Princess murmured under her breath, as she followed the Prince into the light.

*****

"General," the squad leader interrupted, "with all due respect, are we to follow the lead of a junior warrior through the most dangerous traverse in the history of the Pumas? He is but a child!"

There was a low rumble through the gathered Pumas.

The General of the North paused, raised an eyebrow, and turned to the little Prince, who shot to his feet in response, color rising in his cheeks.

"Perhaps you would like to address the squad leader's concerns," the General prompted.

The little Prince almost burst out, but then caught himself. "This is a test of strength," he thought. "It is a test of my pride. If I overreact or reply defensively, it will reveal self-doubts and insecurities. I must be strong."

The little Prince took a deep breath. He knew this squad leader's long-standing doubts about the young warriors. The young warriors had thought long and hard about how to address them.

"Squad leader," began the little Prince, drawing to his full height. "Two moons ago, you were watch commander of the South on the night of the new moon, is that correct?"

The squad leader stood, unaccustomed to such a challenge from one so young. He considered it impertinent, little Prince or not.

"Yes! I was watch commander on that night," he responded, a little too forcefully for the circumstances.

"And, on your 12th circuit, did you not find a falcon's egg on the southwest battlement?" the little Prince asked.

The squad leader's face blanched. "Yes, yes I did. How did you know about that?" he demanded.

"And, after a thorough search that found nothing suspicious, did you not, on your 14th circuit, find a jug of juice on that same battlement?" continued the little Prince, warming to the task.

Color rose in the squad leader's face, embarrassment boiled up in his voice. "Yes! But how do you know these things? I searched everything, everywhere; there was no one there but me!"

"And, after another, even more thorough search that found nothing suspicious, did you not, on your 17th circuit, find bread on that same battlement?" asked the little Prince, a glint of satisfaction building in his eyes.

The squad leader glanced right and left at his peers, who were shocked at the revelations. The squad leader had shared nothing of these matters, even to his closest friends.

"Yes, yes!" he exclaimed. "By the Gods! There was bread there, but no person. I spent until daybreak searching and found nothing and no one! I tell you, no one was there!"

"But, someone was there, squad leader," replied the little Prince. "It was the junior warriors, providing for your breakfast!"

The Pumas erupted in laughter. The squad leader's face turned red, and then he bounced back and forth between the jocular blows from his mates. His embarrassment slowly turned to laughter as he joined in with his friends. He acknowledged the little Prince with a respectful nod, and held up his hand.

When the laughter died down, he announced, "My General, I hereby withdraw my reservations regarding being led by a junior warrior." The Pumas shouted agreement and the little Prince beamed.

The General motioned, and the warriors rose from one knee. He turned to the little Prince and commanded, "Lead on."

*****

The young Princess crept down the passageway towards the royal terrace. The bright light of day illuminated the gauze draperies that separated her from her sister, mother, and father. She could see them now, their silhouettes familiar, but their positions not.

"The King and Queen are in our seats instead of the thrones," she thought. "Time to modify the plan."

She moved closer to the draperies. She gathered her strength, pushing back her fears, preparing for what was to come.

Then she heard a breath. She looked down and saw the sandals of an Inca Warrior straddling hers. He was right behind her.

"This is it!" she thought.

*****

"This is the most difficult part," the little Prince commented casually.

Chapter Eight

The General of the North looked down the rope and watched him reach over and grab the handhold, then release the rope and swing his body over and put his feet in the foot steps. The General tried to not look past the little Prince to the river below.

"I will be clear in a moment, just let me move a handhold or two to the right before you come over," the little Prince added, moving steadily and purposefully, oblivious to the nearly 60-man height.

The General lowered himself down to the transfer position and readied himself. He looked up and reminded the Puma squad leader above, "Two men at a time on the rope, and keep them moving!"

He looked over at the handhold. It seemed impossibly far away and much too small to support his weight. He closed his eyes and reached over. He had always hated heights, but would never let it show; especially to his best friend and the girl he was always chasing up cliffs.

His hand found purchase. Now it was time. He must let go of the rope and pull himself over with one hand while simultaneously locating the two foot steps.

The General took a deep breath and concentrated only on the rock in front of him, blocking out the sun, the height, and his terror. He released the rope.

*****

The Inca warrior grabbed her from behind by the arms and shoved the younger Princess through the gauze draperies, ripping them from their mounts, and knocking over the bordering decorative jars in the process.

She stood blinking in the bright sunlight, the clattering of the jars attracting the attention of the entire terrace.

"My sister!" the elder Princess screamed, jumping up from her seat.

The elder Princess ran to her, chattering loudly. "I was so worried for you! It is so wonderful you are safe! It has been so terrible! The horrible foreigner killed my betrothed! It was hideous! I am so glad you were not here to witness it!"

The elder Princess swept her cape around her younger sister and gave her a full embrace, separating her from the Inca warrior, who stepped back into the passageway, disappearing in the shadows.

The elder Princess held her sister close, her hand running down her back to her younger sister's waist. She gripped the younger Princess's dagger and pulled it free.

Chapter Eight

The younger Princess jumped, saying urgently to her sister in a low voice, "No! Sister! I need that! I need it for the plan!"

"Oh! I am so happy to see you!" her older sister exclaimed loudly, as she hid the dagger in the folds of her clothing. She leaned back into her younger sister's cheek and whispered, "You had your hunt, now I will have mine."

"Come! Sit by me! I need your company desperately after such a trying day! Oh! Whatever happened to your hand?" the elder Princess exclaimed, as she led the younger Princess to the empty seat of the little Prince.

*****

The General looked up from his counting at the sound of a new female voice.

"Administrator!" he barked. "Who is our new arrival?"

"It is the younger Princess," replied the Administrator.

"Oh, lovely!" the General replied, studying the younger Princess as a carnivore does its prey. "There is nothing better after counting treasure than two virgin princesses."

The Queen saw the General eyeing the younger Princess and rose from her seat.

"If you touch them, I will tear out your heart with my hands!" she shouted.

"What on earth is she saying in that babbling tongue?" mocked the General, knowing full well the intent of the message.

"She pointed out that her youngest daughter is already married and warned you that her husband will likely seek revenge," replied the Administrator as casually as he could manage.

"Already married! She is but a young girl! My God! These people are heathens! How can they marry their daughters so young?" the General demanded.

"It is sadly true, dear General. They sell them off as mere children," the Administrator replied. "I will show you."

The Administrator walked to the princesses and the Queen. "Come with me, and do not say a word, no matter what happens. Come with me, now!"

The Queen looked at the King, who gave a slight nod of approval.

Chapter Eight

The Queen and the princesses arose and walked to the throne, trepidation in every step.

"General," the Administrator pointed, "look here." He jabbed the left cheek of the elder Princess. "See this single mark? He then roughly jabbed the younger Princess's left cheek, and then the Queen's. "See the two marks on each cheek? They mark their women. One mark for virgins, two marks for wives. Disgusting, isn't it?"

The General's eyes narrowed as he examined the marks. He turned back down to his counting. "Their ugliness is only accentuated by their marks," he sneered. "Take them away. Their marks sicken me."

The Administrator escorted the Queen and princesses back to their seats, all three rubbing their birth order marks.

"What did you tell him?" asked the Queen.

"I told him that the Queen almost killed her youngest daughter by not telling me where she was. Now, this is your last chance to save him. Where is the young Prince?" he demanded.

*****

The General's right foot slipped again. His left foot scraped against the bare rock but found nothing. His right hand, sweaty and slick, began to slip from the handhold. He raised his right knee higher and searched again with his toes. Finally, he found it. He slid in his foot, put weight onto it, and put his left in the foot step next to it. His knees were bent uncomfortably, but he was alive.

He looked over at the Puma on the rope next to him, whose eyes were as big as condor eggs, and explained, "The cuts are sized for the junior warriors; you need to pull your feet up high to find the steps."

The Puma gulped, and then nodded.

The General looked at him, did his best to appear confident, and said "I will be clear in a moment, just let me move a handhold or two to the right before you come over." It was as close as he could come to imitating the little Prince.

The General turned his head to the right, put his left hand into the handhold and moved his right hand to the next cut.

"If I live through this, I swear I will never leave solid ground again in my life," he thought.

Chapter Eight

The little Prince was waiting for him, already six paces across and nearly a man below down the diagonal way of the Gods.

*****

The Prince edged closer, the steady sound of the clicking growing louder. He shifted his eyes left and right. No one had noticed, no one had detected him. He took one additional short step. Now he could hear him mumble in his strange tongue. It could not wait. It had to be now.

He stepped out into the light and slammed the Inca blade against the foreign General's throat.

"Release them now or he dies!" screamed the Prince.

The clicking stopped, and the gold pieces tumbled back into the chest.

The King rose from his seat and exclaimed, "My son! The Prince!"

The Administrator turned from viewing the battle and said dryly, "So nice of you to finally join us Prince. We've been expecting you."

The Prince shot a look of pure hatred at the Administrator, who smiled flatly in response. It was the last thing the Prince saw before everything went black.

*****

Nearly all the Pumas were on the cliff face. The pace was slow and careful, but steady. One of the last reached across from the rope to the handhold. He gripped the cliff and released the rope, but his right hand was not fully in the handhold. It began to slip immediately.

Desperate, he fished for the foot step with his right foot, but in his panic forgot the message the squad leader gave him at the top of the rope. "The cuts are sized for junior warriors," the squad leader had instructed. "Raise your knees high to find the foot steps."

The Puma's right foot swung back and forth, his search growing larger as his hand slipped further. At the last possible moment, he remembered the instructions. He pulled his knee up, and his right toe felt the edge. His hand slipped out, and he saw the sky.

He was a Puma. He knew the cost. He could not reveal the mission. He could not betray their location. He did not scream.

*****

"You could have been a little quicker, commander!" the General admonished, rubbing his throat.

"My apologies, General," the commander replied. "He did not reveal himself until he attacked."

"Kick him again," commanded the General.

The Prince awoke, his head pounding, and a piercing pain in both sides of his ribs.

"Welcome, Prince," the General called, a genuine smile brightening his face for the first time since his arrival. "Now that you are finally here, we can finish with this horrid excuse for a kingdom and get back before dinner.

"Administrator, inform the Prince of his fate."

The Administrator walked over to the Prince, casting his shadow over him.

"Pick him up!" he commanded of the two Inca guards.

The guards pulled the Prince to his feet. His head felt like it was going to split in pieces, and every move, every breath, brought a brighter, sharper pain to his ribs.

"You dare to disguise yourself as an Inca warrior!" the Administrator shouted in Spanish for the benefit of the foreigners. "You are not an Inca! You do not deserve to wear that disguise!"

"What are you doing here?" demanded the Prince. "Did you sell your soul to them? Did you betray our kingdom for a handful of gold? Is that what you did to your people when you disappeared? Did you betray them for a handful of gold too?"

The Administrator slapped the Prince. The blow brought stars to the Prince's eyes and more pounding to his head. The pains in his ribs passed from sharp to fierce.

"Look down at your chest, brave Prince," the Administrator directed.

The Prince looked down and back up at the Administrator. "What is it?" he asked.

"It is a family heirloom, passed down since my ancestors were judges at the Inquisition," interjected the General, reading the exchange. The Administrator translated the Spanish to Kunzan for the benefit of the Prince.

Chapter Eight

"Like all other devices of the Inquisition, it separates the innocent from the guilty. If you live, you are innocent, if you die, you were guilty," the General smirked.

"The pain you feel in your ribs are two blades. Every time you breathe in they penetrate. Every time you breathe out, they ratchet for the next step. With every breath they penetrate deeper.

"It is very simple. If you do not breathe, you will die. If you breathe, you will die. It is your choice." The General's smile spread across his face, his eyes alight with glee.

"Why?" gasped the Prince. "Why this torture?" Every word brought new pain in his ribs. He could feel the points of the blades penetrating his skin.

"Because, dear Prince," replied the Administrator, "you thwarted the General's last attack."

"I was doing my duty. I was General of the West," groaned the Prince, forcing out the words through the pain.

"Yes, that is true, you were General of the West," replied the Administrator. "But is it customary for Generals to climb down bamboo shafts and fight off attackers?"

"There were no others but me," the Prince replied, each word a battle. He felt the blades between his ribs. He heard them cutting his tissue like a butcher's knife through llama meat. "I sent all my assets to the East. If they breached in the West, we were doomed. It was up to me." He fell to his knees from the pain, as blood spurted from each side of his ribs.

Both of the princesses stood and screamed at the sight of the blood.

"Quiet them, or they die!" yelled the General, incensed at the interruption of his pleasure.

The Administrator turned and glared at the royal family. The Queen turned to her daughters and motioned for them to sit down.

"So, if not for you, the foreigners would have seized the kingdom that day, and we would not be here now, is that correct?" asked the Administrator.

"Yes," the Prince spat out, the word costing him another ratchet of the blades.

"He has admitted it," the Administrator announced to the General in Spanish. "He is the cause of today's events."

Chapter Eight

The General sat back and smiled. "The Ratchet never fails to find the guilty," he ordained serenely.

*****

The little Prince turned his head back to the General of the North and warned, "This is the section I cautioned the Pumas about. I cut this one myself because of the danger. The rock is soft and sandy. You must be very careful here."

The General nodded, hoping that his fear did not show in his eyes.

"I will stay close so you can see my movements," the little Prince continued. "I will stay just one handhold ahead."

The General nodded again, afraid to speak lest his voice crack. His right hand was in the same handhold as the little Prince's left; their feet also shared the same step.

"Watch closely," instructed the little Prince as he moved his right foot to the next step. "The cuts are half distance here, so movements are shorter."

The little Prince put his right foot into the cut and shifted his weight to the right. The foot step broke away, and his right hand slipped out. He was falling.

*****

"So, now that we've finally heard from the brave Prince, we can finish our business here," the General celebrated. "Administrator, explain things to the King."

The Administrator walked over to the King. "There is no sense continuing this, dear King."

"I agree," the King replied. "More death is senseless and will accomplish nothing. Untie the trumpeter, and I will order the surrender."

The Administrator pointed to the bound warrior. He was untied and handed his horn.

The King turned to him and ordered, "Sound the call for surrender."

The trumpeter was crestfallen, ashamed to be the messenger for the end of the Atacameños kingdom. He turned to the East, raised the horn to his lips, and let loose the call, a call he had practiced only once and never in his lifetime ever expected to hear.

Chapter Eight

*****

The General of the North grabbed the little Prince's left wrist with his right hand. The Prince dangled below, swaying gently.

"Hold on!" the General commanded. "I will pull you up! Your left foot will be first!"

The little Prince looked up at the General. "General, do not attempt to swing or lift me, it will only loosen your handhold."

The General looked down and pleaded, "I can save you Prince. I must save you."

"General," the little Prince replied. "I cut those handholds and steps myself. I know them like I know my own hand. I know they cannot hold us both."

*****

The foreign General was pleased. He was pleased for the first time all day.

"Commander!" he cried. "It is time for the virgins, or, in this case, virgin.

"Since you alone among us bloodied your sword today chasing down those runaways, you have earned the right to the virgin.

"Take her here, on the terrace, and make it violent. I want these pigs to be reminded of what we are to them."

The Administrator shot a glance to the Queen. She knew what was coming.

The Queen spoke quietly, "Two." The younger Princess pulled her gaze from the terrifying visage of the advancing foreign commander and looked quickly at her mother. The Queen glanced down at the pedestal between the elder and younger Princess and then back at the younger.

The younger Princess reached out and pulled open the lid of the pedestal. The commander did not notice. He was licking his lips, advancing on her older sister, who rose out of her seat, screaming.

The commander came nearer, now barely two paces away. His eyes were wide, his mouth half open, and his hands were busy unbuttoning his uniform.

Suddenly, the elder Princess reached into the pedestal, scooped up a handful of dream powder, and threw it into the commander's face. He gasped, and doing so, sucked the powder into his nose and mouth.

The effects were instantaneous and overwhelming, as his body had never been exposed to its hallucinogenic effects. His eyes widened, his breathing stopped, he staggered a step forward, then turned around, and faced the General, who appeared as a giant, black beetle in the commander's vision.

Then, the commander's head snapped back, and a ceremonial dagger drew across his neck, slicing it cleanly back to his spine. His blood spurted halfway across the terrace. He collapsed in a heap in front of the elder Princess, her mouth open, the bloody dagger in her right hand.

She looked up from the body to the General and screamed, "You may steal my future, but you will never steal me!" She took the dagger in both hands and drove it into her own heart.

The younger Princess and Queen rose and screamed.

The foreign General stood, pointed to the King, and shrieked, "You shall learn the value of a true man's life! Your kingdom will pay!"

*****

"Hold on!" the General of the North urged. "I can pull you up!"

"General," the little Prince replied. "What is the seventh standing order of a warrior leader?"

"The seventh standing order of a warrior leader is to retain an effective fighting force to ensure the continuance of the names," the General replied, knowing the consequences of his statement.

"General," the little Prince reminded him, "an effective fighting force requires a leader. You are the leader. You are the best of all of us." He looked at the General and smiled.

And then, the little Prince let go. He saw the sky. He did not scream.

*****

"That," the foreign General screamed, pointing to the body of the commander, "is a man! Not an animal like you! Not an animal like all of you!"

The General was face to face with the King, less than a finger away.

"He was worth more than 10 of you, more than 50 of you, more than 100 of you! He was worth 300 of you, and that is how many of you shall die! Three hundred of you! And you will be the first!"

Chapter Eight

The General dragged the King to the dream platform, where the King stood that very morning and received the vision of the condor.

"The morning seems so long ago," the King thought.

The General shoved the King down to his knees and drew his sword.

"Tell him! Tell him!" the General screamed to the Administrator.

The Administrator kneeled down next to the King, while the General paced the terrace seething.

The King lamented, "I have failed my kingdom, I have failed my family, and I have failed the names."

"You did not fail your kingdom, dear King," replied the Administrator, grasping the King's arm. "You made the mistake of all truly civilized men. You assumed your enemy had the same basic human values as yourself. You were met by an enemy who had no value for human life."

"He begs for his life!" the Administrator yelled in Spanish to the General.

"His life is mine!" replied the General.

"You did not fail your family. Let me tell you about failing a family," the Administrator said, emotion building in his voice.

"Six years ago, I took my family into the mountains of the north, where we lived on the run, fighting battles with the foreigners. While I led an army of resistance, my family suffered. While your children grew in the sunshine, mine cowered in the shadows.

"When you defeated the General, he searched us out because of my knowledge of Pukara de Quitor. He killed a quarter of my men in the battle, raped my daughter to death, gave my son to the one they call the Brutus, and gutted my wife before my eyes." The Administrator's eyes were wet with tears, his voice choked with emotion. "Dear King, it is I who failed my family."

He paused, and then looked up to the General.

"He begs to lick your boots and drink your toilet for the chance to learn what a real man is!" the Administrator shouted to the General.

"He will never be a man; he is an animal, an insect, lower than dung!" yelled the General.

"He gave me the choice of coming here and defeating you, or the death of the rest of my men and their families where they stood," the Administrator admitted into the King's ear.

"I came here to save my men's families and to save yours. I traded my share of the treasure for the lives of your wife and children."

The King's eyes widened, and he turned his head slightly to meet the eyes of the Administrator.

"I misjudged you," the King confessed. "I ask your forgiveness for that."

"And you have it," replied the Administrator.

"What shall become of my family?" asked the King.

The Administrator replied, "Your wife will be safe and comfortable for the rest of her life. Your daughter will also be safe with me."

"He offers you his wife and his daughter for his life!" the Administrator shouted to the General.

"They are pigs, as is he!" screamed the General, foam forming at the corners of his lips.

The Administrator leaned closer to the King and promised, "And every year on this day, when the sun turns south, I will bring your daughter here, to this platform, and she will stand and speak the names to the rising sun. She will speak your name. And, she will speak the next name—her own."

The King closed his eyes.

The Administrator stood and announced, "It is time."

The King lowered his chest down onto the platform. The General circled around, holding his sword high.

"For the greater glory of the King and Queen of Spain, and in the name of almighty God!" he cried.

The Prince reached behind his head, screaming in anguish at the pain. The movement ratcheted the blades one more step, and they both pierced his lungs.

The younger Princess and the Queen buried their faces in their hands.

The King saw the sky, then tile, then sky, then tile. On the tile he saw scattered pieces of gold. Then, only sky.

Far above, framed by the blank, blue sky, the King saw a circling condor. It was the condor from his morning's vision.

It was the Condor, the highest deity, the god of two faces, two messages.

The King remembered that in the morning's dream, he thought the face of the Condor was the guardian.

Then, he realized that for him, today, the Condor was the second face, the second message. Today, the Condor was the intermediary between this life and the next.

And, now, it was time for the next.

The Next Name

Postscript

History versus Fiction

This is a work of historical fiction.

It is based on a set of facts related to the Atacameños civilization and its fall.

The Atacameños civilization began about 10000 B.C.E. when hunter gatherers arrived in the area of what is now northern Chile near the borders of Bolivia and Argentina. The society evolved into a multi-class civilization about 1000 B.C.E. and reached its zenith between 1000 and 1500 C.E. In total, the Atacameños civilization lasted 2,500 years, making it one of the longest-lasting continuous civilizations in known history.

The Atacameños civilization was under the influence of, and integrated with, the Tiwanaku civilization from approximately 500 to 1000 C.E. until the Tiwanaku civilization collapsed. The Tiwanaku civilization was centered at Lake Titicaca in modern day Peru and Bolivia and lasted approximately 500 years.

The Atacameños civilization was under the influence of, and integrated with, the Inca Empire from 1450 to 1533 C.E., when the Inca civilization fell to the Spanish. The Inca civilization began approximately 1400 C.E. and ended in 1533 C.E. The Inca civilization was centered in Cusco, Peru, and lasted approximately 133 years.

The Atacameños civilization traded extensively, with contacts and trade goods exchanged with the Amazon basin, modern day northwest Argentina, modern day Bolivia, and modern day Peru. These trading contacts introduced exotic foods, substances, materials, and other goods to the Atacameños, including the hallucinogenic powder used extensively by the ruling and religious classes.

The Atacameños civilization was centered on Pukara de Quitor (Fort or Fortress of Quitor). There is no known record of the fortress being breached or conquered by any opposing force prior to the third battle with the Spanish in 1540.

Postscript

The Spanish suffered two unsuccessful attempts to conquer the Atacameños and defeat the Pukara de Quitor. The first was in 1536 by 100 Spanish under the command of Diego de Almagro. The second was in 1540 by about 150 Spanish under the command of Pedro de Valdivia and Francisco de Aguirre.

Valdivia and Aguirre returned later in 1540 with the addition of a force of Inca slaves, primarily Yanaconas indigenous people. The Yanaconas successfully breached Pukara de Quitor, and the Atacameños were defeated.

After the defeat, the Atacameños leadership and warriors were beheaded—300 in all. The heads were mounted and displayed around Pukara de Quitor. After that day, the oasis was known as "The City of Heads."

The Atacameños civilization formally ceased to exist with the signing of the 1557 Pacification Act.

The ruins of Pukara de Quitor are located in modern day San Pedro de Atacama, Chile.

The dimensions of Pukara de Quitor are:

       Slope: 30 degrees

       Height of north cliff face: 80 meters / 262 feet

       Length: 200 meters / 656 feet

       Width: 120 meters / 394 feet

       Area: 24,000 square meters / 258,464 square feet

Beyond these facts, all characters, characterizations, dialog, actions, and events portrayed in this work are fiction. They do not reflect or represent any person, living or dead, historical figure, place or event.

Notes

Altiplano – The Altiplano (high plain), also known as the Puna, is located in modern day southeastern Peru and western Bolivia. The Altiplano lies at an average elevation of about 3,650 meters / 12,000 feet above sea level.

Bamboo – Climbing poles created by lashing together bamboo and a mangrove root at the top are still used today by pirates in the Straight of Malacca to board and seize container and tanker ships.

Catarpe – Catarpe was the Inca administrative city established about three kilometers / two miles upstream from Pukara de Quitor.

Chicha – Chicha is a fermented drink made from grains or fruits, but most commonly created with corn.

Condor – The Andean condor (Vultur gryphus) is the largest winged flying bird in the world, with wingspans of up to 3.2 meters (10.5 feet). The young are raised on remote ledges and in caves at altitudes above 3,000 meters (10,000 feet), using no nesting material. The white egg measures about 12 cm (4.5 inches) long.

Inca Civilization – The Incas were one of many competing tribes in the area of what is now Cusco (Cuzco), Peru until they rose to prominence under Pachacuti Inca Yupanqui (Pachakuti 'Inka Yupanki) (1438-71), who then adopted the soubriquet, Pachacutec, "Transformer of the Earth."

Pachacutec created the Inca Empire as we know it today. Expansion of the empire, especially to the North, continued under his son Topa Inca Yupanqui (Thupa 'Inka Yupanki) (1471-93). His grandson, Huayna Capac (Wayna Qhapaq) (1493-1525) was born in modern day Ecuador and resided there for long periods while Emperor. At its height, approximately 12,000,000 people were ruled by the Incas.

Huayna Capac died in a massive epidemic that killed up to 50% of the population of the Inca Empire. His two sons, the half brothers Huascar (Washkar 'Inka) (1525-32) and Atahuallpa ('Ataw Wallpa 'Inka) (1532-33), subsequently engaged in a debilitating civil war that severely weakened the Inca economy, society and network of alliances that formed the empire. Atahuallpa eventually prevailed, but ruled a deeply divided and fragile realm.

The Spanish, with about 200 men led by Francisco Pizarro (c. 1475-1541), kidnapped and later killed Atahuallpa, thus effectively ending the Inca Empire in 1533. A series of Emperors were installed by the Spanish in subsequent years. Final guerrilla resistance, most prominently led by Manco Inca Yupanqui (Manqo 'Inka Yupanki) (1533-45), a brother of Huascar who the Spanish installed on the throne as a puppet and later turned rebel, ended in 1572.

In modern times, the Incas are best known for the Inca road and monumental architectural works, such as temples and cities. As a civilization, they were probably one of the earliest adopters of, and most adept at, revisionist history and public relations. The Incas actively suppressed proper attribution of the works and accomplishments of preceding civilizations and contemporary subjugated kingdoms, often claiming those works as their own.

The Incas were also very politically adept. They created their empire by forming alliances among the many competing and conflicting valley and regional powers of the region. Their short-lived civilization was, in many ways, more of a political and trade alliance among dispersed archipelagos than an empire in the classic Western sense.

Llama – The llama (Lama glama) is one of three domesticated forms of the guanaco. All are camelids, members of the camel family, Camelidae (order Artiodactyla). In addition to the llama, the domesticated camelids include the alpaca and vicuña, both bred for their wool. Of the three, the llama is the largest, and is bred for use as a pack animal, as well as a source of leather, wool, meat and tallow. Llamas grow as heavy as 136 kilograms / 300 pounds and average 120 cm / 47 inches at the shoulder.

Metallurgy – The geographical area of the Atacameños civilization is very rich in copper and other minerals. The Atacameños were a Bronze Age civilization, so had no knowledge of, or use of, steel.

Mitimaes – The mitimaes were internally displaced Inca slaves used for agricultural, civic and religious construction projects and general labor in the Inca Empire. It was these slaves who constructed the large scale works that the Incas are most known for in modern times.

Obsidian – Obsidian is a naturally-occurring glass formed by rapidly cooling lava. It is typically black, which was the variety used by the Atacameños to form arrowheads, daggers and other implements. Items were roughly formed by chipping and the razor-sharp edge was created by grinding on a sharpening stone.

Pepper Tree – The pepper tree of the Atacama produces a long pea-like seed pod up to 20 cm / 8 inches in length containing seeds. The seeds were ground into flour by the Atacameños. The pepper tree also features needle-sharp thorns up to 7 cm / 2.75 inches long.

Rape – The rape of virgin brides and the wives and daughters of troublesome subjects was a common practice in parts of the Spanish colonial empire.

Sacrificador – The Sacrificador (sacrificer) was the most feared deity of the Tiwanaku cosmology. The deity was represented with an axe in one hand and a decapitated head in the other.

Sources:

- Pukara de Quitor archeological site and the Museo Arqueologico, both located in San Pedro de Atacama, Chile
- Encyclopedia Britannica 2008
- National Geographic
- Lonely Planet Peru 2007
- Field expeditions to Pukara de Quitor, the Atacama Solar (salt flats), the Bosque de Desierto (forest of the desert) and Cordillera de Sal (salt mountains).

About the Author

Douglas Hackney is an author of fiction and non-fiction books and also writes for periodicals, with over 100 articles and columns to his credit.

Beginning as an award-winning writer at age 13, he became a professional commercial photographer at age 16 and continued a media career that included lead acting roles; modeling; an editor and director of film and video; stage manager; production manager; producer and executive producer.

He subsequently pursued a variety of careers, including microcomputer technology, computer graphics, software, enterprise class computing environments, business intelligence, and technology, marketing, and management consulting.

Mr. Hackney's writing and photography have appeared in a wide and eclectic assortment of books and periodicals, including poetry collections, motorsports, public policy, travel, information technology, and business management.

As a market segment luminary and leader, Mr. Hackney has often been quoted in trade and general business publications, and has participated in more than a score of judging panels for industry awards.

Mr. Hackney served on corporate for- and non-profit boards of directors. He is an award-winning public speaker and has keynoted and chaired industry conferences worldwide.

In addition, Mr. Hackney has lectured regularly at leading MBA programs.

Mr. Hackney holds no undergraduate or graduate degrees, and is self-taught in each of his careers.

Since 2003, Mr. Hackney has been on an extended sabbatical exploring the world with his wife, Stephanie, primarily in developing countries.